Brian Fr… Rhodesia and Cape To… 53. He is now a partner… is his second novel; hi… lly published in 1976 a…

This is h… n:

'A deligh…
Daily Mi…

'A slick fast moving thriller'
Illustrated London News

'Police corruption and the thrill of a car chase – all thoroughly enjoyable'
Police Review

'Hired guns, big money . . . and murder are all here, plus much excitement'
Current Crime

By the same author

Good Luck Mister Cain

BRIAN FREEBORN

Ten Days Mister Cain?

GRANADA
London Toronto Sydney New York

Published by Granada Publishing Limited in 1978
Reprinted 1982

ISBN 0 586 04739 5

First published in Great Britain by
Secker & Warburg Ltd 1977

Granada Publishing Limited
Frogmore, St Albans, Herts AL2 2NF
and
36 Golden Square, London W1R 4AH
515 Madison Avenue, New York, NY 10022, USA
117 York Street, Sydney, NSW 2000, Australia
100 Skyway Avenue, Rexdale, Ontario, M9W 3A6, Canada
61 Beach Road, Auckland, New Zealand

Made and printed in Great Britain by
Hazell Watson & Viney Ltd
Aylesbury, Bucks
Set in Linotype Plantin

For my parents –
welcome home

One

Well you've gotta try haven't you? I mean there I was on this Jumbo burning a slow fuse wondering how I was going to slip past the Heathrow fuzz, when the answer was slumped beside me spitting bother over men in general and me in particular. Not that I had anything to hide at Heathrow. It's just that Old Bill can scent me upwind with a bad dose of nasal catarrh and that makes any contact dodgey. So how *do* you conceal the sharpest criminal brain of the twentieth century from them that get paid to stick the finger up the criminal nose? One thing you don't do is swallow half a pound of cordite and limp like Quasimodo on a crutch. This is a problem requiring what they call finesse. Cheryl-Jo, in the next seat to mine, showed everything I needed. If I wrapped myself in orange barnet, death-dealing lashes and non-stop commercials for the US of A your average law-merchant wouldn't even notice my pixie toes on his size twelves. That was the theory anyway.

Discontent swung heavy on the corners of Cheryl-Jo's mouth and she'd spent most of the flight telling why. Her manner said it was too bad she wasn't married and the louder she hollered the longer she waited because nobody was fool enough to shackle himself to six feet of Long Island larynx whatever the gelt involved. She was wrapped like a Miami widow, which helped. White mink and orange hair make signals to me clear as semaphore to sailors.

Her voice reminded me of a duck turned loose on a sliced loaf. '. . . fraternity-minded jerk. He was so dumb he thought a blow-job was when you got to be referee at a football match.' She swallowed the dregs of a Jack Daniels. 'You gonna buy me another drink? What'd you say your name was?' It's Harry Grant.

'Willie. They've shut the bar. We're coming in to land.'

'Miss!' The hostess came running, knees twinkling under the hem of her skirt. 'The same.'

'Sorry. The bar is closed now.' The shine on the girl's teeth hurt my eyes.

'Closed shit. Bring me two JDs.'

The hostess eyed me for help but I was minding my own interests. 'Same again.'

This chick had nice soft skin but underneath was pure steel. 'Sorry sir. Company policy. The bar closes twenty minutes ahead of touchdown. You can still buy liquor from the trolley to carry out.'

Cheryl-Jo wound her mink tight round her throat. 'Screw the company. Screw you. Get rid of these glasses.'

The bird scooped the glasses like she hadn't heard. I leaned to Cheryl-Jo. 'Never mind, eh? Anything else you want?' I closed my hand over hers. Her nails were painted to match her hair.

'Gotta joint?' She watched my hand till I took it away.

'Not with me, no.'

'Then, Lover, the answer is no. There is nothing else I want.' She frowned. 'What did you say your name was?'

'Willie.'

'You British?'

'English, my love.'

Her eyes glittered. 'If I had a dollar for every pair of balls I'd bust I'd buy Fort Knox. So don't put me on.'

I raised a palm. 'No offence.'

'You speak with a kinda foreign accent, is all. Where you from?'

'Place called Canning Town.'

'Is that near London?'

'Near enough.'

'They use shit in this . . . Canning Town?'

'When the Law's not looking.'

She yawned. 'You scared of cops, Willie?'

'Right.'

'I guess you never did anything wrong in your whole life, am I right? Your Momma let you smoke shit, sweetheart?'

'Not till my third birthday.'

Thing is, America's stiff with chicks like this. Some berk slips them a joint at a party and they ponce about like Public Enemy Number One, breaking the law every Saturday night.

'Anyway,' she was going on, 'if this Canning Town's near London I guess you know London City pretty good?'

'Good enough.'

She sat up. 'OK, Lover. You just got yourself a job.'

'How's that?'

She was stuffing books and sweaters into an ox-blood bag.

'Showing the sights to Cheryl-Jo. You'll like that.'

'What's it worth?'

She was going to curse till I unpeeled the lust in my eyes. 'British, American, they're all the same,' she sneered. 'Wait and see, Stud. If you're a real good guide maybe Cheryl-Jo'll give you a chance to show you're the greatest in other departments.'

'Bingo.'

She was having a punch-up with her luggage. Cussing, bracelets jangling, she dragged a brown paper parcel out of her ox-blood bag. 'Stinking bag.' She zipped up and scowled at the parcel on her lap. 'Do me a favour, Stud.' She tossed the parcel at me. 'Stick that in your luggage till we get to unpack, right?' I reached my overnight bag off the rack. It was half-full and took the parcel easy. I closed the zip and balanced the bag on my knees. 'Pigskin. Set me back seventy-five dollars.'

She closed her eyes. 'Chickenshit.'

I scanned the bag for a bit, then glanced at my watch. Cheryl-Jo opened her eyes as I stood. 'Wash,' I tucked the bag under my arm. 'Bit of a shave. Gotta say hullo with a clean jaw.' She didn't shift as I squeezed past.

Inside the carsie I sat on the bog-lid and took her parcel out of my bag, turning it in my hands. Soft. I slit it open and grinned at the polythene bags inside. Getting stoned of a Saturday night was all very well between friends but carrying your grass through Customs was obviously something else. You needed a stooge. There must've been three pounds of it, sealed in six separate polythene bags. I sat quiet and watched the situation change. When I was in the Smoke last grass was fetching sixteen quid an ounce and no bother, twenty if you struck lucky, but I'd be looking for a quick sale. It was time to change course. I rummaged through the pigskin. I'd tucked over a hundred Tampa Nuggets at the bottom on account of I'm partial to a good cigar and didn't fancy English prices for a while. Then there was the rolled-gold pen I'd bought in LA. Not much cop for HM Customs but it would irritate the bejesus out of them if I flashed it round the manor, and HM Customs are not famous for their patience. A bottle or two would round the catch off just nice. I shaved quick at the basin and tucked a polythene bag into each pocket of my suit, six in all. Then I smoothed my jacket, checked my tie and stepped out of the carsie. The hostess was scraping plastic cutlery into a hopper. I cleared my throat.

'Can I help you, sir?'

'Well . . . is it too late to buy liquor?'

She frowned. 'Vicky is unloading the trolley right now.'

'I know.' I ran a hand through my hair. 'Look, I'm dead sorry. The lady with me, she asked me if I could get . . .' She sighed and led me to Vicky. 'What had you in mind?' I picked off two bottles of bourbon for a start. 'Got any gin?'

'British Customs allow only one bottle of hard liquor per passenger, sir.'

'I know.' I winked. 'We've made friends with a couple of teetotallers back there. Thanks. And a bottle of brandy. Ta.' I paid and she started to pack the booze into plastic carrier-bags. I rearranged them and strolled back to my seat carrying a bottle of mother's in one bag, and two bourbons a gin and a brandy in the other.

Cheryl-Jo looked up when I dangled the heavy bag in front of her. 'Present from Uncle Willie.' It made a pretty sight, all those bottles shining through transparent plastic. 'To make you fancy him strong.' I sat down and tucked the bag under her seat.

She was sour. 'How old did you say you were?'

'Very. Your mascara's spreading, Doll-face.'

It didn't take long. After a couple or three dabs at her face she took a toilet bag from her hand-luggage and stood up. I waited till she reached the carsie then slipped the booze out of her carrier-bag and pressed one of the packets of grass into the bottom of the bag. The four bottles went on top. There was no way you could see the grass unless you took the booze out. When Cheryl-Jo got back her make-up was perfect, the lights were flashing and the hostess was checking the seat-belts.

The plane bounced twice and reversed throttle with a noise like God on Sunday. Then we were taxi-ing to the end of one of the piers. Seat buckles clattered as the passengers unwrapped their legs and reached for their clobber, checking the day through the portholes. The sun slopped in the puddles on the tarmac and a blast of cold air brought the citizens to their feet and fighting for the door. I scooped the pigskin off the rack and lifted both carrier-bags with my free hand. Cheryl-Jo looked suspicious as I tucked a hand under her elbow and steered her down the aisle. The hostess stood at the door, feet together and hands folded, warming all with the Standard Smile and hoping they'd had a good flight. Except Cheryl-Jo. Then the sun stroked my eyes and I was breathing spring air. It was like shrugging into an old overcoat.

But Cheryl-Jo was rabbitting again. The way she figured I could get her settled at the Inn on the Park before heading back to Canning City for the rest of the day. She'd see me next morning at nine-thirty and we'd do a little shopping in this Knightsbridge; then if the day went good I could introduce her to Tramp in the evening. By this time we'd reached the Immigration Hall.

'Listen,' I told her, 'we gotta divi for a while. See where it says UK Passports? I go through there on account of I'm English. You go through that one.' I pointed. 'See you on the other side, OK? Want me to carry your bag?' She nodded and I doddled up to the desk. I flipped over the little blue book, chuffed by the steadiness of my own hand, and tried to suss what Friend of Fuzz was thinking under his cap. Did he eye my jacket pockets? Then he snapped the passport shut and shifted his gaze to the feller behind. I was through and waiting for Cheryl-Jo.

I reckoned I cut a distinguished figure lounging there in my velvet suit, so I fished out a cigar and lit up to complete the effect, unbuttoning my jacket while I leaned against a pillar. Cheryl-Jo's barnet was bright as the sun in the aliens' queue. The line moved slow till she faced the fuzz at the desk. Your aliens take longer and I could see questions and answers batting back and forth like a natter down the nick, Cheryl-Jo's hair crackling aggro as the minutes ticked by. Then she was out, one hand stuffed with papers, eyebrows knotted.

'You know what that mother-fucker asked me?' I didn't but she was going to tell me. 'He asked did I have sufficient funds for my vacation. Me. I said where I come from people stand on their own two feet and no citizen of the United States is gonna show her face anyplace unless she can be sure she will not besmirch the reputation of America by applying for Welfare on vacation.' She stopped for breath and I grabbed her arm.

'He's probably never met a Daughter of the Revolution before.'

She shook my hand off. 'Pretty fucking funny.'

'One more gate.'

She beat my ears with words all the way up the escalator.

We waited in the mob round the carousel at the top. Cheryl-Jo tapped a rhythm with her foot as the cases heaved through the rubber curtains and wobbled round the conveyor. I scouted about and found two trolleys. Cheryl-Jo pointed an orange nail. 'There.' I picked off an ox-blood suitcase just as I saw my own. It could've been dodgy, but today God had come out in support of villains. The label had been torn off. I set it on the spare trolley. Cheryl-Jo's case had been the smallest of a family which I stacked careful on her trolley.

'I'm through,' she said. 'Let's split.'

I hung her carrier-bag on the handle of her trolley, watching the four bottles swing, then pushed both trolleys towards HM Customs. Along the way I wound her up and let her go as the gates came in sight, so by the time we arrived she was spraying the walls with words hard as shot. I steered her to the green gate which said 'Nothing to Declare', nodding sympathy and giving her charge of her trolley and its bottles, peeling off towards the red section on my own. She paused and I smiled.

'Same as before. See you on the other side.'

She shrugged and wheeled out of sight.

I breathed deep and hooked on my John Citizen face, the one that says I need help because I'm just not used to all this. The customs officer was an old bloke, greying sideburns showing under his cap, but then any blue uniform inside fifty yards gets the corpuscles running relays up my legs. He leaned his knuckles on the counter.

'Sir?'

I smiled, desperate to please. 'I've got . . . something to declare, haven't I?' He watched me scratch in my hand-luggage, spreading toilet-bag, a sweater and a copy of *Playboy* on the counter. 'Sorry.' I dropped four packets of Tampa Nuggets and let the blood fill my face when I picked them up. 'More here. Somewhere.' I turned the pigskin upside down and scattered another sixteen packets. 'Cigars,' I told him. He watched me crawl about, dropping them fast as I picked them up.

'Is that all, sir?'

'No. No, it's not all.' I laid the pen beside the cigars. It fell off the counter. 'Then there's . . .' I stood the carrier-bag in front. 'Gin.' I stepped back like a con waiting for the cuffs. 'That's . . . it.'

'Sure?'

'Um . . . yes.'

He nodded and I could see him thinking why me. Of all the fuzz doing a hard day's pinch at Heathrow why does the biggest berk have to choose me?

'Well, sir.' He sighed, pushing the sweater, toilet bag and *Playboy* to one side. 'I suggest you put those away. They're duty-free, you see.'

I mumbled sorry.

'I'd gotta take them out to show . . .'

He stopped me with a look. 'Yes.' He counted the cigars, setting the allowance on one side. 'Put those away too. Was there anything else?'

I had the sweater tangled round the handle of the pigskin. 'The gin?'

He hooked a finger through the loops on the carrier-bag and dangled it over the desk. 'How many bottles do you see? Sir?'

'One.'

'Just so. And how many bottles of spirits are we allowed to bring into the United Kingdom free of duty?'

'Er . . .'

'One. Sir.' He dropped the booze on the counter.

'Go on.' I grinned, embarrassed. 'What about . . .' I pointed at the pen.

He looked at it like I'd fished it out of the S-bend. 'Tell you what sir.' He beckoned me close. 'If you promise not to tell anybody I promise I won't.'

I looked at my feet. 'Thanks.'

I paid for the cigars and he wrote out a receipt while I got my gear together. I dropped the *Playboy* again as I reached the doors.

The outer hall echoed with calls for flights and the screams of kids too young to die. I battled through the crowd till I stood facing the exit from the green section. The doors snapped open as a couple came through and I glimpsed Cheryl-Jo, orange hair burning between two customs officers. One of them had a tight grip on her arm. I picked my luggage off the trolley and carved a path towards the exit.

Two

Outside the puddles were drying under the wheels of the taxis and buses. I had a butcher's up and down the kerb and saw him leaning on his cab reading the *Daily Mirror*.

'Crab.'

His head snapped up and I swallowed my shock. He'd turned into an old man in nine months, smaller and thinner than ever, strips of grey spreading through smooth black hair. His razor rash had spread from his jaw, winning the fight for his cheekbones, and his eyes had sunk so far all you could see was shadow. I dropped my case and grabbed his shoulders, fingers sinking into cloth.

'How you been?'

'Harry.' His hand was cold and his eyes were focused on my left shoulder. 'Nice to see you.'

I stepped back, hands on hips. 'You haven't been getting proper dinners, mate.'

He nearly smiled. 'You ready then?'

I stowed my bags and climbed in the back. 'Home, James. I couldn't half do with a pint.'

Crab started the motor, pushed through the traffic and did a U-turn round the pick-up island. I fished out a packet of Nuggets and lit up, leaning back in the seat with my hands behind my head.

'How you been, then? How's business?'

The back of his neck looked nervous. 'So-so. No complaints.'

'Great.' I leaned forward. 'Have a cigar. Tampa Nuggets. You can't get them here.'

He looked over his shoulder as we neared the tunnel. 'No, ta.'

'Go on. Take one.' I emptied the packet. 'Tell you what . . . take the lot.' I shoved them over his shoulder. 'From me to you.'

'No. Honest.' He blocked them with the back of his hand. I shrugged and dropped them back in the packet.

'Suit yourself. You oughta see the States, you know. It's worth it.' I leaned near the window. 'See this?' I pinched my lapel. 'No, go on, feel it.' Crab raised yellowed fingers, one hand on the wheel and eyes on the road. 'A hundred and ninety dollars. The shirt? Forty. Pure silk. And hand-made shoes, look. It's a whole new ball-game over there, you can live like bloody royalty.' I fell back in the seat as the taxi swayed round the circle and up the incline to the motorway. It was all green, grey and black. Small-looking motors hummed past from the West while we stuck behind National Carriers in the slow lane. The cab was moving nervily. I sat and watched the houses getting denser, turning into factories as we got near Brentford and Chiswick.

I blew smoke at the driver's window. 'I can honestly say I made a success of it. I've got nearly a grand in my pockets not counting what I scored at the airport and a couple more in a safe place back in New York.' Well, a bit of exaggeration never hurt anybody yet. 'Dollars, of course.' I dragged the polythene bags out of my pockets and dropped them in the pigskin. 'Where's the best market for grass these days?'

The cab wobbled. 'What, drugs?'

I'd forgotten. 'Well . . . not your *actual* junk, no. None of your hard stuff. I mean you can't call a drop of grass drugs, can you?'

Crab faced the blacktop again. 'Dunno. I dunno anything about that.'

'You mean you don't know the market?'

'No.'

The cab was on the Chiswick flyover skimming past fourth-floor windows and peeling adverts for Smith's Crisps and Lucozade. Brentford Nylons in red neon. A few spots of rain fell on the windscreen and Crab worked the wipers before he needed. They swished a couple or three cycles then started to grunt on the dry glass. It was true what the Americans said about the English. They didn't like success. They resented successful men; wished them bad.

'So.' Crab's shoulders twitched at my voice. 'What's this job then?'

He pulled the lobe of his ear as we stopped at the first set of lights. 'Well . . . it's pretty big.'

'It better. It's not every day you can drag a bloke three thousand miles for . . . chickenshit. What's it about? I wouldn't've come for just anybody, you know.'

'I appreciate that, Harry.'

I wished he'd turn the wipers off. 'So what's it about?'

'Look.' We joined the one-way system at Hammersmith. New glass buildings poking through grimed brickwork. 'Don't ask me too much, eh? I can't say much without the others, know what I mean?'

'Anybody I know?'

The motors in the Cromwell Road were thicker than ever.

'Nobody you know. No.'

'From up West?'

'Er, no. In actual fact they're from outside the Smoke altogether.'

I sighed. 'Christ Albloodymighty. He drags me three thousand miles for a mix-up with a bunch of fucking swedes. Bloody roll on. Would it be putting you to too much bother, I mean, would it cause an unacceptable strain on your medulla oblongata for you to inform me exactly where these swedes come from?'

I waited. 'Newcastle. Look, Harry, don't . . .'

I sat up. 'I might've known it. Some bloody Scotch mob. Don't know A from a bull's foot, that lot, take it from me. It's all haggis and sodding bagpipes up there you know.'

' 'Tisn't Scotch.' Crab showed a flash of the old spark. 'It's

Geordie.'

'I just hope you know what you're doing. And for Christ's sake turn your wipers off.'

The birds in High Street Ken seemed to've grown longer legs since I was there last. But Biba had gone quiet.

Crab spoke again as we came up the Piccadilly underpass.

'Best keep the questions till tomorrow, Harry, OK? I'll introduce you then.' He tried to grin over his shoulder. 'You won't be sorry.'

'I'm already sorry.'

'Wasn't easy getting you in, you know.'

'Where's my gaff then?'

'Charlotte Street.'

We went the rest of the way saying nothing. Fitzroy Street hadn't changed. The North end, as you enter from the square, is lined with newish offices but as you get further down into Charlotte Street you start to smell the Greek caffs, all charcoal and herbs and foreign music trickling on to the pavements. A few nutters were sitting at the tables outside tucked into their overcoats waiting for retsina but mostly the mob on the pavements was Greeks doing business or English going somewhere else. I noticed Schmidt's was closed up.

We stopped outside a run-down tobacconist's. Crab nipped into the shop and came out with a middle-aged party wearing National Health specs and eyebrows like Groucho Marx.

'Harry Grant. This is Mr Bishop.'

We shook hands and Bishop unlocked the door next to the shop. He spoke to Crab like I was deaf and dumb. 'Where's his luggage?'

Crab opened the taxi and started unloading. Bishop stroked me with his eyebrows and led us into a hall about three feet wide and up a flight of stairs that shook like jelly at Christmas. I cussed as I tripped on the landing.

'I got news for you, Bishop. Over in the States they use a funny new system, all little wires that give off a sorta bright fire . . .'

Bishop nudged a time-switch and I wished he hadn't. 'Christ

I liked it better in the dark.'

The lino was torn and working loose on the treads, and the walls hadn't been painted since Charlie Chaplin left the Old Kent Road. Bishop, breathing heavy, poked at a lock on the top floor and leaned on the door. I stepped in and dropped my case with a thump that bounced the furniture.

The gaff was one room with a kitchenette and a bathroom leading off one side. The roof sloped into the walls at three feet off the floor and the windows were the dormer type down the end of short tunnels through the roof-space. I scanned the string showing through the carpet and the scratches on the Shirley Temple furniture.

'Fallen are the mighty.'

There was a single bed jammed in the corner next to the door, two ton of dark brown dining-table and one old arm-chair showing the cushion stuffing. A wardrobe and dressing table stood like soldiers against the wall opposite the bed. Bishop held out the keys. 'Twenty a week. In advance.'

I cocked an eye round the room. 'You'll be lucky.'

'Your mate here already agreed.'

'He was robbed.'

Bishop's eyebrows touched his hair. 'I wouldn't 've bothered to clean up if I'd known.'

'Christ. What was it like before?' I tested the springs on the bed.

Crab shuffled. 'It *is* sort of . . . central, Harry.'

'Fifteen.' I had a wallet and two pockets to support.

'Eighteen-fifty.' Bishop rammed his fists into his cardigan pockets.

'Seventeen.'

He managed to clasp his fingers through his cardigan. 'So break me. Seventeen. In advance.'

I'd brought forty-odd quid with me so as not to get caught short and I counted seventeen readies into his hand. He dropped the keys into my palm. 'Good luck, Mr Grant.'

'Merry Christmas.' I shut the door after him.

Crab was shuffling again. 'Well, if that's it Harry, I'll . . .'

'Hang about.' There was a coin-box phone on the landing.

'You better take my number.' He scribbled it in a notebook. 'See you when?'

'Tomorrow.' He walked backwards. 'Call you about eleven, OK?'

I bit a cigar. 'Right.' I wondered if the smoke from Tampa Nuggets killed bugs.

'Er . . . cheers, then.' He fumbled for the balustrade. 'Cheerio.'

'Mind how you go.'

I shut the door and listened to him patter down the stairs. He'd forgotten to ask for his fare.

I reckoned if I was out early enough next morning I could have a bit of a wander and be back at the gaff in time for Crab, so first thing I doddled into the weak sunshine and sliced a track through Greeks and delivery vans into Oxford Street. It was just short of nine and the road was streaming like a sewer with citizens falling off buses, bubbling up the tube steps and panting into nasty offices for the day's pickings. Like I said it was spring and just coming on mild so a couple or three of the bolder birds had shed their outer layers to prove themselves women again. After all, six months is a long time to leave blokes wondering. I called into a caff half-way along and sat at a plastic bar drinking Nescafé with a dried bun, watching the mob on the pavement. The chick behind the counter was done up like Miss World with a little white cap instead of a crown and seeing that she wasn't that busy we had a talk between scrapes of the Stork. She said she was resting between engagements which I took to mean like the chorus line at the London Palladium but she said no, fiancés, she had this thing about getting engaged. I swallowed my coffee, got her phone number and shouldered out into the crowd.

Take Six is a smooth place, all quiet carpet and lights that claw your eyes. I had a sniff about for the suit I'd seen in the window, cream suède looking soft enough for nappies, and wasn't disappointed. It fitted a treat, and although eighty nicker hurt right now I'd be laughing once Crab showed with his gang of swedes. The salesman broke out in a sweat when I tried to pay in dollars so I went and changed some bread to spare his glands. I got a taxi back to Charlotte Street and left my gear on the bed while I nipped down to Tesco in Goodge Street. A jar of Nescafé, a few tins of this and that and I was ready to hustle Fanny Craddock if she was still about the manor. The only gap was a crate of Light and another bottle of mother's. I thought I'd wait for Crab first.

I left the door open so I could see the phone on the landing, but by half-eleven I wasn't going to sit watching any longer. Crab's number was in my old black book.

'Hullo?' A woman's voice.

'Crab there?'

'Who?'

I'd never met Crab's missus but I knew from way back that she did not warm to the sound of the phone, being inclined to regard Al Bell's baby as an invention of demons or at least an operation masterminded by the Law for the purpose of keeping tabs on her old man. She was not therefore one to prevaricate when joining a round of electronic bunny. So I asked this bird the number and she said it right so I asked her who she was and she said Mislash which did not sound like Mrs Crab. I asked the address and she gave it right. Then she wanted to know where I'd seen her card and did I have time to come round. She was going on something strong when I put the phone down.

All of which caused me more than a few aggravated thoughts. If Crab had moved why hadn't he said? Forgot, maybe, but meantime here was I waiting on another man's pleasure which I do not regard as my true function in the Universal Plan. In fact it was getting up my nose. To work off my lather I found a broom in the kitchenette and set to on the layers of dust round the gaff. It wasn't nice but by one o'clock the place looked more like a flat than a horse-box. Then I stowed my gear in the wardrobe, careful to put the grass under the shirts in a drawer. By that time my gut was beating tattoos on my ribs so I boiled a tin of spaghetti in one of

Bishop's saucepans and ate it on toast. With black Nescafé and the tar from a Tampa Nugget in my blood I felt more like a mensch.

I put my feet up and considered what to do. First, the Major. Crab, the Major and me had pulled more deals together than I'd had cold looks from the Law and if anybody had kept the finger on Crab's backbone it would be the Major. Easier decided than done. I dialled seven different numbers before I found him.

He sounded chuffed. 'Harry old boy. When did you get back?'

'Yesterday. You're as easy to find as the Invisible Bloody Man, you know that?'

'Sorry,' he laughed, embarrassed. 'Discretion, y'know. Necessary.'

'Anyway. All right, are you?'

'The rudest of rude. I say, I do wish you'd let me know you were coming home. I could have used a man with your talents.'

I perked up. 'What, this Newcastle job? In with Crab are you?'

'Newcastle?' He paused. 'My dear chap, I banished the entire North-East thirty years ago. And I haven't seen Crab for five months. No, my thoughts are far from Newcastle, far, even, from the Sceptred Isle.' He dropped his voice. 'Beirut. I leave this evening.'

'Oh. Stopping long?'

'A few days.'

'Flogging . . . tractor parts again?'

He laughed. 'We must meet for a snifter when I get back.'

'Right.' I gave him my number.

About two I dressed in my suèdes and did a couple of spins at the mirror to make sure they looked the same as in the shop. The mirror was grisly as a lag in a leper colony, coming out in black spots, so I couldn't really tell. Down in the shop Bishop was hunched over the Woodbines like a hawk with a rabbit.

'I wanna new mirror,' I told him.

'For seventeen quid I want the old one back.'

'Old one?' I looked puzzled. 'Where's that then? I mean, there's this modernistic portrait in back of the closet door? All spots and stuff . . . ?'

'Seen your type before,' he sneered. 'Go over there and get all Yankyized and come back thinking you know it all.'

'Told you that, did he?'

'I'm busy.' He turned his back.

'Oy.' I said it soft but the tone never fails. 'He leave a phone number or something? An address?'

His eyebrows lifted so slow I thought his lids would collapse under the weight. 'Who?'

'Crab.'

'Crab who?'

I sighed. 'You're just anti-American. The taxi-driver. I mean the bloke that brought me.'

'No.'

'No what? Bananas?'

'No he didn't. Leave a number. Nor an address either.' He shifted packets of fags from one shelf to the other. 'I'm busy.'

'So you said.' I watched him. 'What did he do when he booked the gaff?'

'Do?' He frowned. 'He just came in and booked it.'

'How?'

'Cash.'

I laughed. 'In advance, right? So I'm a fortnight in hand.'

'Like buggery.' Bishop waved an arm and knocked down a tin of St Bruno. 'He paid three days. Half a week.'

'Remind me you owe me ten nicker. And he didn't tell you where you could reach him?'

Bishop was glad to change the subject. 'Didn't need to. Just came in here and paid three days in advance. Said he'd see me on the day. Didn't even look at the room.'

'That figures.' I turned. 'Don't forget my mirror.'

Mislash. It might just be Crab done up in leather drag and getting charvered by swedes too pissed to notice. And of course it was always possible old Crab had sussed a score using a brass for window-dressing, sniffing through the customers' pockets while she drew blood with her bangles. I crossed Oxford Street and into Wardour Street, turning left past Young's Dress Hire with the dummy brides grinning rigid in the windows. Further down the movie men still plastered their showcases with stills from the pictures, fighting for air with recording studios, boozers, and record shops blasting the dust off the pavement with pop. I turned into St Anne's Court. At least, it had been St Anne's Court. Someone had pulled down one side, leaving the North terrace shivering like a bird in a shower when the water stops. It was that unfamiliar in the sunshine I had bother sorting out the gaff. I found the door and searched the bells for Crab. 'Beautiful Model', 'French Lessons', or just 'Walk Up' but no Crab. Miss Lash was there all right, top floor where Crab used to muck with his missus. The front door was open so I took the stairs two at a time.

Crab's door was painted shimmering pink and the handle shone like the Eddystone Light. I opened slow. Soft lights, a carpet to match the colour of the door, and on old hen doing a crossword at a curly table. She looked up. 'Hullo, dear.' If this was Miss Lash it must be early closing day. 'She'll be a few minutes. Like a drink while you wait?'

I winked. 'No, ta,' strolled across the carpet and opened the door at the end while the old biddy, seeing all was not what she'd expected, yelped loud enough to wake Ginger Marks.

'Albert!'

She was too late. There was Miss Lash wearing a bow tie and rings on her fingers playing horsey on some berk with his wrists tied to the bed-post. It was like a tableau at Madame Tussaud's only the customer was hairy. Anyway, neither of them looked like Crab to me and I was bowing out when a hand like a foot fell on my shoulder and chucked me on the carpet, followed by a welted size ten (patent leather) which connected somewhere near my breast pocket. I was on my feet and looking for the door when Albert, ugly as Igor and twice as big, reached for my cream suède collar. Seeing him pass the point of no return I did the only thing I could, which was to grip the old bird's jumper and, sort of, interpose her body between us. They hit the carpet with a crash that dropped an autographed picture of Gloria Swanson on Albert's loaf. Last I heard on my way down the stairs was the old dear's wail changing tone like bagpipes warming up for a gig. Crab had definitely changed his address, and him a controlled tenant. I dusted myself down outside. I'd have hated to meet Albert when he was narked.

There's a feller called Scotch that runs a club in a Dean Street basement and I'd have called in there to sink a snort and bash the bunny anyway. Half-way down the steps the smell brought it all back; gin and polished wood, sweat, and smoke-drenched velvet. But that wasn't all. The crackle in the air told you this was where you'd get your chance if you were smart enough to recognize it. I stood at the bottom of the stairs waiting for my eyes to catch up, listening to the clink of glass. The bar looked the same, mirror washed in red light from below, silhouetting the barman.

'Scotch.'

I knew it wasn't before he turned. The bloke facing me was tall as Scotch but twenty years younger and much less lovable.

'Sorry. Thought you was Scotch.'

'I'm not.'

The thing about the English is their warmth. 'No.' We inspected each other. 'Give us a drop of mother's, will you?'

He looked so hard I wondered if Albert had left a trademark on the otherwise pleasing regularity of my features.

'Fifty.' He set down a tumbler.

'Gone up?'

'No.'

'Cheers then.' He moved off. 'Where is he?'

'Who?'

'Scotch.'

'Out the back.'

'Tell him I want to see him.'

He turned to the sink. 'He's having a kip.'

'Tell him Harry Grant's back. He'll crow like a cockerel.'

The barman shrugged and picked a path across the floor to a door between a pair of booths. Light scythed the murk. I leaned an elbow on the counter and felt for my cigars. Albert's boot had found bullseye; they looked like a packet of brown boomerangs. I was trying to break one in half when the barman came back. A minute ago he'd been unfriendly but now he looked like Eichmann giving readings from the Talmud.

'Scotch isn't well. He can't see anybody.'

I was losing my sense of humour. Eichmann stepped aside just in time.

Scotch was playing patience under the light of a desk-lamp, papers and books piled on the edges of the table. The room was warm and damp and a blanket lay rumpled on a couch at the back. He half-stood, wiping his palms on his sweater. His pose made me think of a gorilla with piles, and my aggro fizzled.

'Scotch?'

'It's OK, George.' He winked over my shoulder. 'Let him be.' George backed off and shut the door while Scotch cracked his face for me. 'Harry. When'd you get back?'

'Yesterday. What's going on, you punchy old sod?'

He ran a hand like a side of beef through spikey grey hair. 'Ah, you don't wanna take notice. I never knew you was back, thought it was some herbert coming the old moody.' He was still looking at the door. 'How are you?'

I dropped into a chair. 'Fine.' Well, his nose was still bust but everything else had changed. 'Streets paved with gold in America.'

'Yeah?'

'That's where it's at, Mac.'

'Yeah?'

It was like talking to yourself only I give myself better answers. 'Made a few bob. Not a fortune, but you could say I'm kinda comfortable.'

'Good.'

He wasn't even going to offer me a drink. 'Seen Crab?'

'Who?'

The next jerk that said who like that was going to cop a

drop of knuckle. 'Crab.'

'No. No I haven't.'

'Well when did you?' I waited. 'Scotch. I said when did you see him last?'

He wiped his mouth. 'Musta been a coupla months. Yeah. Maybe three. He came for a quick jar.'

'Did he say he'd moved?'

'No.' His face was crumpled as a duster. 'Never saw too much of him after you left, and that's the truth. In actual fact not much of the old mob come round these days. Not like the old times. Nobody you'd wanna know these days.'

'Not surprised.'

I stood and straight away he was limping to the door. 'Nice to see you.'

'I'll drop by again. Maybe tomorrow, eh?'

He stopped. 'None of the old mob come round nowadays.'

'So you said.' I blocked the door.

'These are bad times, Harry, bad times.' His hand was heavy on my shoulder. 'I wish you hadn't come back, honest to Christ I do.'

'Leave off. You'll have me in tears.' I opened the door.

The drizzle in Dean Street varnished the road and dripped off the street signs. I ought to have bought a coat. It was turning parky.

Three

I was already feeling the lack of wheels so in the morning I caught a fourteen bus down the Fulham Road to suss the motors at Frankie's. Now Crab and Frankie had been muckers in the Scrubs at one time and kept tabs pretty regular so you might say my reasons for visiting were twofold. The bomb site had run down a bit, if that's possible. The flags on the fence looked tatty, showing threads at the edges and oil-stains on the colours. I crunched over the cinders to the wooden hut at the back. It was like a steam-bath in there with the paraffin heater but Frankie sat in his overcoat and titfer minding his loot. He didn't recognize me.

'Help you, Squire?'

'I'll help myself.' I stared at him. 'It's me, you daft bugger.'

He blinked. 'Harry.'

'The same. How's trade?'

'Bit rough at the edges.' He fiddled with a pencil.

I pulled out a chair and sat facing him but he stood up and started flipping through a calendar on the wall. 'I need a jam-jar for about five quid and I don't buy unless I get Green Shield stamps,' I told him.

He pushed his hat back on his head and scribbled on a pad. 'Lemme see. You had the forty-two Stud, right?' He looked very sad. 'Nothing like that now. I don't deal in that end of the market no more. Specialist stuff, that is. Sorry. Standard cars, quick turnover, no messing.' He had his face close to his exercise book.

'I'll have a look about, OK?'

He looked up. 'I'm telling you. You won't find anything you fancy.'

He was drawing little arrows on his pad.

'I'll decide that.'

'I don't wanna waste your time, Harry. There's a bloke near Lillie Road might be able to help you. He carries a lot of your kind of motor.'

'I'll have a shufti anyway.' My stomach was trying to tell me something.

I strolled down the concrete path while Frankie leaned on the doorpost, hands in his overcoat pockets. Minis, a Renault, a couple of Volvos – even an old Sunbeam. I leaned on a bonnet, watching Frankie watch me. Well, I'd laid it on since I got back, I mean you don't want your mates thinking you're a failure do you, and the truth was my pockets were that light I'd be lucky to afford a Vespa unless Crab showed soon. But Frankie didn't know that. So when I saw this Pontiac, big as a Christmas tank, I patted it. The tag on the windscreen said four-fifty.

'Give you four if it works.' I had to shout.

'Not for sale.'

'Turn it in, you berk. It says four-fifty.'

'It's sold.' He trod down the path, shoulders hunched, Robin Hood brim masking his eyes. 'Sold this morning. Four-fifty.'

'Who to? Trade?'

'Punter.'

'Bloody hell didn't he take it with him then?'

'Coming back tomorrow.' The windscreen distorted the reflection of his face. 'Told you there was nothing you'd fancy. Try Wolfendens. Down by Lillie Road.'

'Why didn't you take the tag off?' My voice was soft.

'Gimme a chance. He only left ten minutes before you come.'

'Give you five ton.'

'Can't. It's sold.'

And that buttoned it up. A year ago he'd have flogged it to me and conned the punter out of a tenner for all the bother he'd gone to. I walked round the bonnet and beckoned him close.

'Seen Crab?'

'What?'

'Never mind.' I walked towards the gate.

He called out. 'Harry. Don't take on like that. I tried to tell you.'

I skimmed down the Fulham Road like a con let loose on his birthday. The English were getting me down. I must've forgotten what it was like.

Wolfenden's was a skip this side of Lillie Road. They'd knocked the fronts out of three Victorian shops and glazed them, the cars standing in tight ranks on the forecourt. By the time the bloke with the leather elbows came out I knew what I could afford. A 1962 Austin 1300 resprayed black with a white stripe down each side.

'How much?'

Leather Elbows opened the driver's door. 'Hundred and fifty.'

'Let's have a spin.'

He fetched the keys from the showroom. There was only thirty thousand on the clock, which was suspicious, but she acted like it was true. When we got back I was ready to buy.

'One-twenty.'

'One-forty.'

'Jack? Tools?'

'All there.'

'MOT?'

'Till January.'

'One thirty.'

It was all over in five minutes. He came out with the log-book and MOT Certificate.

'She's taxed till next month.' He leaned on the window, confidential. 'Don't forget to . . .'

'Thanks.'

I nearly took his leathers with me.

The Sunroom is in Old Compton Street over a clip-joint a hundred yards West of the Charing Cross Road. It was thick with Georgie Farmer's lot at one time till old Georgie carved a pair of cavalry he thought were on the payroll. I mean, you can carve who you like as long as you pay their wages but even the fuzz get bitter being sliced for nothing. Anyway Georgie went down for ten and the Sunroom hasn't been the same since. The gaffer was a spade called Sonny who had a record long as a chorus girl's legs laid end to end. He'd stopped open in the old days by feeding fivers to Old Bill and copped a spot of bother when they had a shake-up down the Yard. By the time I left for the States he'd been shut down twice in eighteen months. Still, after Georgie bought this package tour to the Isle of Wight Sonny played it soft and the Sunroom got quite healthy. Good steady custom, no rubbish and no inter-firm punch-ups. And it was a useful manor when your wallet was thin as mine. If I scored early Crab could go whistle for all I cared.

There was a brass leaning on the door downstairs which surprised me on account of it being dinner-time and not exactly thronged with punters. She hoisted a hip across the passage as if to say you're welcome so I smacked her bum, being mindful of the lads limbering up behind the door, splitting tables with their hands for laughs.

'That'll cost twenty pee.'

I tripped on the stairs because she had a bloke's voice, and come to think of it her arse was very hard.

'Ever heard of Consumer Protection?'

'Money's all you think about.' He flounced. 'Blue Eyes. All you can raise is a mortgage.'

'Come up and see me. When you've had a shave.'

The doors on the landing swung open and a brace of spades blocked the way. When I heeled about and looked again there was only one but he was wide as twelve.

'How do. Where's Sonny?' I was panting.

The spade fingered his bow-tie. 'Why the noise man?'

'Just a friendly slap-and-tickle. Where's Sonny?'

'Running Brixton. What's your business?'

I lit a cigar but it was no competition for the smoke rolling through the doors from the Sunroom. 'I'm an old mate. Came for a game. Meeting a bloke called Crab.'

He fanned the smoke with a pink palm. 'Crab?'

'Little bloke. Looks like a bandleader. You remember.'

'Crab, is it?' He nodded. 'I know the man. Hasn't been by for a month or two.' He stepped back, holding the doors with a foot. 'You better wait inside.'

The Sunroom is a cave about fifteen feet high with ceilings panelled like a Lyon's Corner House. There were four snooker tables, each sweating under its own light. The table at the end stood apart, flanked by three tiers of benches. The championship table, not that Joe Davis was expected that afternoon. The bar stood at the far end next to a counter where Sonny used to collect the subs. The spade looked in the membership book.

'What's your name?'

'Harry Grant.'

He ran his finger down the page. 'This book says your membership nine months overdue, man.'

'Been away, haven't I?'

'Four pound. And it's fifty pee a game if you wanna play.'

He took the money. 'This other cat. Crab.' He folded his arms on the book. 'You tell him this. I don't like the company I see him keep last time.'

'How's that, Goldilocks?'

'You tell him.'

I shrugged and ambled to the bar. They'd even changed the barmaid. This one looked like she'd just got up. I bought a quick one.

'Have a drink?' I was being polite.

'Bacardi and Coke.' She did sums in her head and gave me the change without a sniff at the Bacardi.

'Well,' I raised my glass. 'Don't get stoned, will you, love?'

'No. I'll get rich though.'

'Just remember I helped, OK?'

A couple of fellers stood in the smoke watching the game at the first table so I lurked round the edge looking for a friendly face. A bloke poked his head into the light, cuing up on the black near the centre pocket. He wore a beret, and scarlet braces over a short-sleeved pullover with a line of Christmas trees round the waist. The black clunked and skidded down the baize while the feller with the braces muttered and pulled back into the dark, fingers chalking the end of his cue. His mate picked a fag off the edge where it smouldered on the varnish, took a drag and squinted down the table. He shook his head, walked round the end and sussed the situation from the other side. A fast line-up and the black smacked into the corner pocket. Then he flicked the score-pointer with his cue and lifted his pint off the shelf while the party with the braces counted readies into his spare hand. The audience scattered and I moved on down the hall.

I saw nobody I knew so I found a seat on the bottom bench near the championship table which at that moment was not graced by champions. I suppose the game was all right, good accurate stuff without much excitement, but it wasn't exactly League standard. Anyway, it was nearly finished. I'd sat there a while when my shoulder-blades started twitching. When I turned all I saw was a pair of zip-up boots with stacked heels.

'Harry?'

I said, 'Well.'

You wouldn't invite Shiv Lacey home to tea but I was getting partial to anyone who didn't dial doomsday soon as he saw my boat. He was a thin lad, very tall, dressed in a tight black suit and a fancy waistcoat. If you asked me old Shiv watched too many Westerns but that wasn't the kind of thing you said to his face. He was twenty-three years old.

'Have a drink?'

I nodded. 'Gilbey's.'

He eased off the top bench like Jack Palance slipping off his horse, waistcoat glinting in the light. His hair was snow-white, always had been, thick and waved over his ears. They called him Shiv because they said he was handy with a blade, a rumour most folk tried not to test. What you don't know can't hurt you. Or so they said. The thing was, Shiv Lacey had what you might call a volatile temperament and for that reason most firms up West stopped out of his way. I mean, if you're running a firm you've got to trust your soldiers not to lob mortars at mosquitoes and with Lacey you couldn't be sure. His eyes told you he'd flick the blade if you hiccupped. Last I'd heard he'd latched on to some new mob South of the river, a bunch of heavies with more smash than grab, but that had been more than a year ago so maybe he was back on the beat. The game was finished by the time he fetched the drinks back.

'Fancy a flutter?'

'Why not?' He didn't know I was near skint, after all.

I flipped half a bar and he went to pay the spade while I set the table up. Then he took his jacket off and laid it flat on the top bench so it wouldn't get dirty. He wore arm-bands on his shirt-sleeves and granite on his face.

'Twenty-five a point?' He took a cue from the rack and sighted down the stem while I felt my pockets.

'Suits me.'

Lacey returned the cue and took another. 'Haven't seen you for a bit.'

'No.' I found the chalk dangling at the end of the table. He tossed a coin. 'Heads.'

'So it is. Break.'

I was out of practice and smashed the pyramid too hard, but today must've been St Hustler's Day because one of the reds dropped into the corner pocket. I hoped he didn't take it personal.

'Luck.'

He watched me sight the green and I was almost pleased when it hissed wide.

He leaned into the light. 'Haven't been up West for some time.' He sank a red.

'Where's your manor now then?' I watched him drop the pink. My pockets felt lighter. 'South, is it?' He twitched and sent his second red off-course. Something was tickling his trigger-finger and I hoped he wasn't due for one of his turns.

'Not any more.'

'Eh?'

'Not South any more.'

I got my head down and sent another red home, then the brown which was teetering anyway. Lacey fancied himself at cards so I thought I'd shift his mind to happier days.

'Ever call in at that new place in Streatham, what was its name, the Alhambra?' I picked a likely-looking red.

'Once.'

I missed. 'Any good?'

'It's a fit-up.'

Sorry I spoke. Lacey leaned along the table and started smashing them down one after the other.

'D'you remember a bloke called Crab?'

He glanced up. 'Ugly little bugger?'

'That's him. Seen him lately?'

'No.' He moved the score-pointer, totting up his winnings while I had a quiet panic. 'Why? You don't deal with prats like that, do you?' He showed his teeth and I wasn't sure I liked them.

'I was. Waste of time.' I tried a fancy stance, gave up and fetched the rest. Missed again.

'You're . . .' he dropped a red, leaving four on the table, 'in the market then?'

I was casual. 'Could be.'

He sank the blue and walked round the table, dropping his gaze close to the surface. 'I was going to say . . .' he pocketed another, 'if you're in the market I might have something to interest you.'

'Go on.'

'When I've skinned you.'

It didn't take long and I reckoned I was lucky to drop as little as seven-fifty. Even that hurt. It was time to start groping for gravy.

'After that the least you can do is buy me another drink.' He shrugged into his black jacket and fetched a couple more glasses.

'I'll be moving soon.'

'How d'you mean, moving?'

'Up North.'

'Where?'

'North.' He sipped his scotch, panning dead eyes on my face. 'Thing is, I got married.'

'You never.'

A group at the middle table cheered at some clever bit of work I couldn't see. Lacey's eyelid flicked but he didn't turn his head.

'So I wanna get away, know what I mean? Somewhere new.'

Oh well I thought, another career ruined. 'Like haggis, do you?'

'So I need a few bob, don't I?'

I laughed. 'Don't look at me, mate . . .'

His elbows stuck out like coat-hangers as he felt in his pockets and pulled out a wad of tissue paper. A bracelet. A bracelet crusted with sparklers that caught the light like little beacons. I touched it.

'What's it worth?'

'Legit? About seven and a half ton.'

'Give over.' I scanned it hard. 'It's so hot it's charred the paper. Seven-fifty in Hatton Garden maybe, but the way you're holding it you won't gross a penny over one-fifty, straight up.' I turned my back on the room and inspected the sparklers in the flame of Lacey's lighter. I'd seen enough in my time to know it was genuine, and anyway the heat in my pockets told me so. 'You know the buyers better than me.' I dropped it in his palm. 'Why don't you flog it?'

'Can't. Not up West.'

I nodded. 'Listen sweetheart. You just told me it's got nuisance value on top of everything else. What makes you think I'm so keen to lose an arm or a leg?'

His eyelid twitched. 'You've got time to suss the market.'

'No chance.' I lit a cigar and watched the smoke settle on the light.

Lacey burrowed in his right pocket. 'This change your mind?'

A ruby big as an egg on a silver chain.

'Christ.'

'So?'

Well, I'd come to the Sunroom to suss the pickings, hadn't I? I had no more than a hundred and fifty left.

'Give you ninety for the bracelet.'

'Chickenshit.'

'You watch too much television,' I snapped.

He shook his head. 'I can't come out with less than a hundred and fifty, and that's giving it away.'

'Look,' I said, 'when are yóu going?'

He gazed into the gloom. 'Soon as I've got the readies together.'

'Well I can't take both at once. I'll give you a hundred on the nail for the bracelet, right? Then if you're still around I'll come back for the ruby.'

He swallowed his scotch. 'Time you get back I'll be in . . . Aberdeen, or somewhere.'

'Maybe.' I blew a smoke-ring. 'But you've gotta be careful who you flog it to, haven't you?'

His lips were white. 'I'll take the hundred. Now.'

It was a dodgy business. Fifty nicker left in my pocket and no place to flog the sparklers. One thing was sure, I wouldn't be hawking them up and down Old Compton Street. This situation demanded headwork. I gave him the hundred and dropped the tissue parcel in my pocket.

'Give us your address in case I come back for the ruby.' He gave me a number in Dartmouth Park Road. As we pushed through the doors I tapped him on the shoulder.

'Where's the market for grass these days?'

'*You're* asking *me*?'

'Forget it.'

We said goodbye on the pavement. The drag-queen was still posing in the hallway waiting for a fare.

Four

Royal College Street isn't what it used to be and for the herberts that live there that's lucky. Maybe stations used to be trendy or maybe they just needed to keep the workers handy, whatever the reason the whole manor North-West of St Pancras must've been spawned by the railway between a shunt and a crank, miles of flat-faced terraces where the herberts lived and drank and thumped the missus while the soot settled on the walls. Your only chance those days was to nip up West and score a bob putting the leathers into a Nigel or three, Nigels being more distinctive then on account of their top hats. The situation got blacker with the brickwork until the time when the krauts started bouncing Krupp's Easter Eggs off the slates, thereby letting the light through a few holes. The citizens scanned what was left, told themselves the krauts were right and started carving up the rest. Then they built the same thing only cleaner.

Up the North end the street is much the same as it was, Victorian shops and flats both sides, badly run-down, and of course the shops are nowhere compared to Bond Street but a glance shows all the trades you need. Secondhand beds leer through windows at tailors and moneylenders, grocers and timber-merchants; the boozers play bouzouki or jigs and there's a massage parlour amazed it's not in Frith Street. But the busiest part is the crossing with Camden Road. That's where the railway rides on thirty-foot cast-iron columns, showing a belly with rivets like an attack of measles. Past the crossing the tracks march straight as an army all the way to St Pancras on brick arches, and under these arches you find a thousand trades hustling for a living with damp below and trains above.

I turned right just before the junction and followed the viaduct past a timber-yard and a plumber's merchant. The railway runs diagonally to the streets so the further you drive the more space you've got between the arches and the pavement. D. Kalinikou had nicked about fifteen yards which he'd fenced with corrugated iron high enough to turn off all villains under five-foot-six, which in that manor accounts for most. A sign-board swung over the gates, painted by Kalinikou himself with more bottle than style, 'Scrap Metall'. I parked on a yellow line and had a butcher's up and down, snagging my trousers on the bits of wire dribbling through the fence. The gates shook like cymbals as a train whooped and crashed past in the direction of Newcastle. Inside the yard was piled with old silencers, tin baths, copper pipes and sheets of whitened lead, leaving just enough room to manoeuvre the Bedford parked close to the brickwork. Kalinikou had two arches which he'd panelled with bits of iron from the yard and painted primrose, leaving a window so he could suss the visitors when the Bedford wasn't blocking the view. He'd painted his name again above the window, starting bold on the left and ending squashed like a boxer's nose when he ran out of space. The door was a sheet of ply on a wooden frame with a padlock big as a fist. I unhooked the chain and stepped inside.

The brickwork was lime-green and glistening with damp. Condensation and smoke combined formed a fug thicker than either which was just as well since it clouded the underside of the arch and stopped you worrying about the trains. There was another partition about twelve feet back which locked away most of the depth of the arch, and Kalinikou sat at a table in the corner, telephone clamped to his ear while he scribbled on a pad. He didn't recognize me but that wasn't amazing since I'd only met him once and that had been five years back. He waved me to a chair piled with newspaper while he jabbered in Greek, and it wasn't till I moved the papers that I saw the dog chained in the corner. He stood still as stone, ears flat and nose pointing at my gut, feet astride a bowl of water. I made a kind of good-boy sound and pixied round the sides of the room while the hair on his neck lifted silent and straight. I sat down out of reach. Me and the dog looked at each other. Then Kalinikou hung up.

'Yes-my-friend?'

He was a short bloke with a chest like a bull and black hair that greased his shirt collar. The hair on his wrist covered his watch-strap, and he used his hands in two sweeps to clear most of the junk on the table. I offered a cigar.

'Remember me?'

He dismissed the cigar with a pack of Turkish which explained why the room smelt like an Istanbul cat-house. He was the only feller I ever met that could operate a Zippo lighter to get a flame in one stroke.

'No.'

'Dennis, isn't it?'

He fanned the smoke. 'Demis.'

'Yeah.' I set my right ankle on my left knee, being careful not to crease my trousers. 'We did a deal, four, maybe five years ago. Harry Grant.'

A thick finger stabbed the cumulus hanging over the table. 'Harry Grant. Sure. We make a deal with the ladies' wear.' He shook my hand. 'The frocks and the knickers.'

'The same.'

He rocked in his chair, hands splayed on the table, fag getting wet between his teeth. 'Ha. How's the tricks?'

'Still in the same line, are you?'

He stepped to a kitchen cupboard in the corner behind the dog. The dog's ears pricked and he melted under Kalinikou's feet, rolling goo-goo eyeballs like a lamb but he didn't fool me. Kalinikou lifted an unlabelled bottle two-thirds full of clear liquid with one clouded tumbler and what looked like a jam-jar. He faced me with arms spread.

'Raki.' The glasses clinked. 'Have a drink.' He slammed the bottle on the table. I didn't like the look of the marks on the glass, I mean a million germs can live and work in a single tide-mark, but then I was grateful he kept the jam-jar for himself. Anyway, the invitation was more in the nature of an order and I didn't want to rock the boat.

He poured half a glass.

'Cheers.' I coughed. No germ could survive that stuff.

He gulped, smacked his lips and picked a hair off the rim of the jar. 'So. More business?'

I fished Lacey's package from my pocket and opened the paper on the table. The surroundings gave it even more class, like a deb in a transport caff. The sparklers glowed like Boston harbour on the fourth of July.

Kalinikou whistled. 'Christ. Where you get this?' He reached into a drawer under the table and raised a magnifying glass, hands gentle as petals as he fingered the bracelet. 'How many stones?'

'I didn't stop to count.'

He set it on the tissue paper and finished his raki. 'Where you find this?'

'Bloke I know. What d'you reckon to it?'

He shrugged. 'A buyer. No problem. I find. But Harry, this is dangerous, huh? How long on the market now?'

'I reckon less than a week.'

'Not too bad.' He coughed, keeping his fag in one corner of his mouth. 'But I need time. Something like this, you don't sell tomorrow. You understand?' He filled his jar and shoved the bottle towards me.

'That's your problem. How much?' I topped up my glass.

'Is worth . . .' he picked it up, 'maybe five hundred pounds. I must sell for . . . I dunno . . . four hundred, perhaps less because I must move it quick, huh?' He scratched his scalp. 'I give you . . . one-fifty.'

Well you've got to read between the lines, haven't you? If he said five ton he meant seven or eight so four hundred meant about six. By that reckoning I oughta be making a good two and a half ton out of it.

'That's too bad.' I sipped my raki. 'I was looking for more like three-fifty.'

He snorted. 'Harry. No jokes. Please.'

'No joke, Dennis. I need three-fifty or it's not worth my while.'

He waited while a train passed overhead. 'Can't do.'

'Please yourself. Don't tell me you're not going to flog it for six ton yourself. I'm offering you a fair margin.'

He laughed. 'Two hundred. Top price.'

'No way, Pussycat.' I drank. 'Listen. I've got more if you're interested. You like rubies?'

'Rubies?'

'What I'm saying Dennis is this could be the tip of the iceberg if you play straight with me now.'

'Two-fifty.'

'Look.' The dog growled when I leaned forward. 'I'm only working on a percentage. I gotta hit a reasonable margin otherwise it just isn't on. I'll take my bloody rubies somewhere else.'

Kalinikou rasped his stubble with his knuckles, elbows making dents in the pad on his table. 'I like you, Harry. You are the straight guy.'

'Sure. I'm Father Christmas.'

'I make a proposition. I help you if you help me, OK?'

'Tell.'

'I give you three hundred . . .' he ground out his fag, 'if you do me a favour.' He pulled out a key. 'Come.' I followed him to the door in the partition. He kicked the dog aside, unlocked the door and switched on a light. 'Come.' I tip-toed round the dog. The room at the back was about thirty feet long, a continuation of the arch over his office only the far end was bricked up. There was a porcelain sink in one corner and two shelves above piled with stacks of old newspapers. The floor was piled with cartons. 'So.' Kalinikou waved an arm. 'Smirnoff vodka. Sixty dozen bottles. All fell from the lorry, no breakages.' His laugh echoed round the vault.

I was impressed but I didn't see how I could help him with sixty dozen bottles of firewater unless I laid it in store and drank myself daft for the next five years. Anyway I couldn't afford it and told him so. He laughed again.

'I don't want you for buying. I want you to help sell, OK?'

He turned to the door. 'Come.'

We stepped into the office and I sat down while he locked up. Then he perched on the edge of the table and poured another raki.

'Now you ask yourself how you help.' He wiped his mouth with the hairs on the back of his hand. 'I have a buyer. A good man. I know him well, we do the deals for years. Now. Sixty dozen bottles I have. But my friend, he needs only forty dozen. So, you sell twenty dozen I give you three hundred pounds for the bracelet. Is a deal?'

'Sod off.' I was thinking hard.

Kalinikou shrugged. 'All right. No deal, two hundred for the bracelet.'

I was in no position to ignore a chance. There had to be a few bob in this if I could figure the wrinkles.

'Smirnoff retails around three-fifty a bottle. How much does your friend pay?'

'Twelve quids one case.'

'You happy with that?'

He shrugged. 'I'm a businessman. Is what you get these days.'

'Yeah. No, what I'm saying is, if I can get you only . . . say, ten quid a case, will you take it?'

He wagged a finger like a log. 'Bloody English. I get ten quid and Mr Grant makes two, huh?'

'You're not as daft as you look.'

'No. Twelve pound a case.'

'Jesus Christ . . .'

'Twelve pound one case.'

'Don't blame me if I can't sell, then.' I raised my glass. 'Cheerio.'

'Twelve quid? You agree?'

I shrugged. 'No choice.'

He smashed his jam-jar against my glass. 'This will be the start of beautiful friends, am-I-right?'

'I'm beautiful already.' We drank. 'Suppose I can get you, say, one-thirty a bottle for the whole sixty dozen?'

Condensation dripped on the table as a train belted past.

Kalinikou shook his head. 'I sell to my friend.'

'In love are you?'

'Harry.' He looked serious. 'Forty dozen is not for talking. Is sold to my friend. Finish.' He knifed the fug with the edge of his hand.

'That's what I mean.' I considered him. 'Love before money. You must like him to lose that much. I mean, I dunno, I might get . . . one-fifty a bottle. That's another three hundred and sixty quid. Fifty-fifty of course.'

'No.'

'So when are you delivering to Lover-boy?'

'The day after tomorrow. Why?'

'Just a thought. Do me a favour. Don't deliver till you hear from me, OK?'

Kalinikou folded his arms across his chest. 'Harry. No deals. No tricks.'

I raised a palm. 'Stay cool, Adonis. I wouldn't dream of wrecking your marriage. But there might be a way of making a few bob on top if your mate will play ball.'

'How?'

I raised a finger. 'Leave it to Beaver. No tricks. Your mate gets his forty dozen at a quid a throw. Trust each other, do you? I mean, on top of loving each other?' He smashed his chest with a fist like a rock. 'We are friends for years. Family friends. He is from Crete.' He pushed his stubble close to my face. 'I play no tricks on my customers.' He thought. 'Well . . . I play no tricks on my friends. Or Cretans.'

'Very wise.'

He walked me to the gate.

'Dennis, listen.'

'Huh?'

'You ever meet a feller name of Crab?'

'Crab?' He pronounced it 'Crub'.

'Skinny little party. Used to run a taxi.'

'Crab? I don't . . .'

'Didn't think so.' We doddled to the 1300 and I stood with a hand on the door. 'Where can I flog an ounce or two of grass?'

'Grass?' A train roared overhead. 'The marijuana?'

'You got it.'

He shrugged. 'Myself, I don't handle.' He ran his fingers through his hair. 'I heard one time there was a . . . syndicate?'

'Yeah?'

'Export-import. South of the river. I can find out for you. You want me to ask?'

I shook my head. 'This isn't syndicate stuff. I need a street-merchant or somebody.'

'Sorry.'

I climbed into the car. 'See you tomorrow. Remember what I said, don't touch those bottles till I get back.'

On the way home my brain was turning faster than a spin-drier on a Monday morning. Like I said there'd gotta be a quid or three in this for anybody with a drop of the old one-two. And yours truly was blessed with more than just a drop.

Five

I was kicking the kerb outside the Wardour Street branch of Rymans when they opened at nine. There was a rack showing packets of Blick stickers, with a catalogue of available shapes drawn on the back of each packet. A number 1218, white, looked about right. There were 175 stickers to the packet so I did some sums and collected five packets. I didn't see the plastic kind so I asked the chick at the cash desk.

'Plastic?' She frowned. 'No. Try our Portland Street branch. Sasco.'

'Eh?'

'Sasco. The stickers are called Sasco.'

Rymans in Portland Street is like a Waitrose flogging stationery instead of cornflakes. I found the Sasco packets, choosing a white vinyl disc maybe five-sixteenths in diameter. They came in packets of 220 so I bought four. Then I collected the car and drove to Kalinikou's gaff.

Kalinikou was twiddling the hairs on his chest and leading off at the phone in Greek. I pointed at the back door and he wedged the phone on his shoulder long enough to drop the key on the table. I walked round the dog and let myself into the back. Sixty cartons of Smirnoff stood bold and drinkable around the walls. I broke one open. Twelve metal caps poked through the packing.

'So?' Kalinikou looked in.

'Help me get the packing out.' I took off my jacket and we spread papier-mâché and shavings on the floor till twenty cartons showed loose bottles.

'You have the buyer?'

'I know where to go.'

'Why you take out the packings?'

'See these?' I showed him the vinyl stickers. 'Stick one dead centre on each bottle cap. So. OK?'

'Why?'

I coughed on a cigar. 'Price tabs. And bottles with price tabs have always been unpacked. Now do you wanna make some bread or not? I'm not keeping you up, am I?'

He grunted and did as he was told. Working together it took twenty minutes to cover the two hundred and forty caps.

'Now the Blick tabs. Fill in the price on each one. Three pounds fifty.' I waited while he scribbled, then started smoothing the completed price tabs over the plastic discs. It took half an hour because it had to be done so the discs underneath didn't show.

'There then.'

Kalinikou frowned. 'Why we have the plastic underneath?'

'Patience, baby, patience.' We stepped into the office. 'I'll need the Bedford. Got any spare registration plates?'

He raised his eyebrows as if to say 'what a question' and dug out his collection from the back room.

'Which one you like?'

I dropped the recent ones. 'These. F was 1967, wasn't it?' We swopped the plates on the Bedford in five minutes, him at the back and me at the front. 'Let's load.' We carried out the cartons two at a time till the twenty were piled on the concrete at the back of the van. Then he passed them up to me. When they were stacked neat I jumped down and locked the van doors. 'Where's my jacket?' He followed me into the office and out again. 'Remember what I said. Leave the rest till I get back.' I tossed my jacket onto the passenger seat and dragged off my tie.

'Where you are going?'

I patted his whiskers. 'A long way from here, don't you

panic, sweetie.' I chucked my tie in and messed my hair before climbing behind the wheel. The Bedford puffed blue smoke and lurched through the gates. 'See you later.' Kalinikou waved.

The van fell short of a Bentley for speed and comfort. Every inch of tarmac was dragged out of the cylinders in a series of explosions that shook the vodka into cocktails. Through Camden Town I leaned an elbow on the window and joined the secret brotherhood where cabbies and truck-drivers waved you on instead of playing kamikaze. I nearly bit my tongue as a filth-waggon lurched at the lights when I raced the amber but the cavalry were just giving up their right of way.

I've been South of the river maybe a dozen times in my life and driving over Waterloo Bridge I remembered why. For a start the buildings look foreign. Course, I'd got used to the Festival Hall – you can see it from Victoria Embankment – but since I'd been away they'd started ferreting round East of the bridge as well, leaving a pile of concrete bands hanging over the river like a loose deck of cards. I turned right at the Circus, street map open on my jacket, and into Lambeth Road where I realized I could've come straight over Lambeth Bridge. Still, on safari better stick to tracks you know.

Then there's the people. They're not the same. Straight up, a lot of them remind me of the herberts on the streets when I was a nipper, like somebody had held the clock still. You half expect to see queues with ration-books. And as you turn down Kennington Park Road there are birds pushing prams which is something you never see up West, I don't know why. And the place names. Course some names are enough to lay the horrors on Burke and Hare, I mean you can't expect to read a sign saying 'Wandsworth' without getting lumps behind the ears, but the rest just don't sound English. Camberwell might as well be Uskadar and Blackheath's a home for gnomes. Clapham and Balham are a disease or a comedy team, and Tooting is the first sign of a bad bout of Bec. But queerest of all is Streatham. I've always said if God meant it to be pronounced Strettam he'd have spelled it so. But Streatham it had to be.

The further from home the better.

Mind you, like I'd told Lacey, I'd only heard about this mob secondhand so of course by rolling down there I was risking a score paid in ice-cream and popcorn. I was beginning to wish I'd asked Lacey more when I had the chance. Anyway, since they ran the only bank South of the river likely to nod at what I was peddling I didn't have much choice, did I?

Streatham High Road is as foreign as the rest of the manor only more so. It's a double carriageway with flowers in the middle and is therefore extra wide, letting in the sky and making you wonder if there's desert behind the supermarkets. Then you realize that between Tescos, Boots and the Co-op, the Bingo halls and penny arcades stand blank and waiting for dark. It wasn't a bother coasting the Bedford down the East carriageway since most of the motors were on the other side heading North, it being about half-eleven. This casino had once been a dance palais where birds in floppy frocks without tits would glide with blokes in patent leather hair to the sound of Victor Silvester, but all that ended with the War. It had been empty for years, then used as a Bingo hall till the present firm had converted it into a casino just before I left for the States. The Alhambra, they called it, and it was already outselling the rest of the street within a fortnight of the Gala Opening. I did a U-turn at the lights and joined the stream going North, peeling off into the quiet of the nearset side-street. I tied my tie, combed my hair and put my jacket on before tucking a carton under my arm and crossing the street to suss the place from the opposite side. A curly stone canopy stuck out over the pavement and the three-storey face behind was draped with neon tubes like dried spaghetti. I reckoned the whole front turned into a Spanish castle at the flick of a switch. You had to admire them. A Spanish castle in Streatham High Road showed imagination. I doddled back to the crossing and waited for the lights checking the cut of my suit in the window of a caff while I stood. I figured I had the class to match theirs.

One of the Spanish doors under the canopy was ajar so I

leaned hard and fell into the lobby on account of it was lighter than it looked. I was facing another arch, this time with a portcullis whose spikes would make a nasty dent in anything daft enough to hang about come closing time. It was half up so I ducked underneath. The old dance hall had been thirty feet high and maybe a hundred feet square and I was standing on the edge of a Spanish courtyard that would've had Darryl F. Zanuck choking on his cigar. Balconies, windows, trellis-work, turrets – even PVC creepers up the walls. The floor was stone flags but round the tables lay deep white carpets, each one the size of a flock of sheep waiting for rain. You couldn't help being impressed.

A feller thumped out of a side door. It's not all wine and doublets in Streatham, I could tell. He stopped when he saw me, then built up speed like a tank, heels pounding the stone till I thought he wasn't going to stop in time. He wasn't too accurate, his nose was flattened, and his breathing was heavy. An old pug.

'Got an appointment?'

'No.' I pointed at the carton under my arm. 'Guv'nor in?'

'You want an appointment.' The scars over his eyes were horrible. 'He don't see nobody without an appointment.'

I selected a cigar and let the smoke trickle through my nostrils. 'He'll want to see me. Tell him I've got a couple or three bottles he might be interested in.'

He wasn't too bright, the pug. He scratched his head, wondering whether to deal a row of knuckles or do like I'd said. Then he turned himself round and lurched in the direction he'd just come from. I strolled over, bathing the manor in careless abandon in spite of the chill in my shoes. I'd got halfway when the pug chuffed out followed by one of the fattest geezers I've even seen. Everything on him wobbled and he walked with his feet splayed like he'd got kicked in the crutch by a mule. He wore black trousers like tarpaulins and an evening shirt open at the neck, bow tie hanging like string down his chest. He hadn't shaved and he showed black under the eyes. Next time anybody tells me fat blokes are jolly I'll snuff him on the snout because I've met some serpents in my time but this was the king and ancestor of them all. His eyes were bloodshot and wrapped in folds of flesh. He wasn't breathing heavy. In fact I doubt he was breathing at all.

'What is your business?' He watched the carton under my arm.

I chewed a cigar. 'I was just telling your mate Dempsey, I got something you'll want to see.'

'What's your name?'

I locked my eyes on the fringe of his bald patch. 'Willie. Willie Griffin.'

'Where are you from?'

'Newcastle.' Straight questions deserve bent answers.

He looked at a watch on a strap the size of an army belt. 'All right, Willie.' The weight of his cheeks dragged at his mouth. 'I am an easy-going sort of bloke. Good sense of fun, know what I mean? Now if you have failed to make me laugh within two minutes from now I shall get Percy to show you out.'

The pug twitched a shoulder and whistled stupid through his teeth.

I tapped the carton. 'Smirnoff. Twenty dozen bottles.' He wasn't even smiling. 'For you, cheap.' Dealing with parties like that is like handling a mad dog; you've gotta show them you're not scared or they'll bite your leg off for laughs. Fat Man was running his marbles over my suit and cuff-links. He nodded at Percy.

'OK.'

The pug blinked and wheeled away like a bulldozer on one track. Fat Man looked at his watch again.

'Come inside. Bring that.'

I followed him across the paving to a set of doors marked 'Theatre Barcelona' in black iron letters.

It was like stepping forward four hundred years. A small auditorium, maybe fifty tip-up seats upholstered in green velvet facing drapes that shone gold in a spotlight. Fat Man waddled to the front row and crashed into a seat. He loosened his waistband and waved me to the centre of the row.

'Hang about. Gotta check this first.' He nodded at a feller standing in the aisle. 'Let it go.'

I dropped the carton under a seat as the lights went down and music shook the walls. The drapes parted and a pink spot pierced the dark.

Well, I've charvered some chicks in my time but this one sent the hormones on hunger marches. Everything from the disdain in her eyes to the silver on her heels said this was no Billingsgate scrubber. She wore a blue floor-length gown rippling purple in the light, ash-blonde hair piled high on her head, and a row of sparklers at her throat that might've blinded a lesser man. The music wasn't raucous but it had a rhythm you felt through the seat and she knew every stroke. The bloke in the aisle called out:

'Now, duckie, don't leave it too late.' He had the voice of a boy-wonder in a cathedral choir.

The bird made no sign she'd heard but eased centre front, peeling first one glove then the other which she trailed over the satin on her belly and dropped at my knees. She turned her back, scarlet nails probing for the zip at her nape which she drew slow, the blue parting like an arrow to the cleft of her buttocks. Then she stepped warm and supple out of the gown.

Some fellers excuse ugly birds by saying they're warm-hearted. If looks mean cool this chick's soul must've been pure Arctic. She faced the seats. Her skin was covered in a silver powder that caught the light like oil. It was like she'd heard my thoughts because she dropped her chin and caught my eye before spilling her bra in my lap.

Fat Man spoke. 'This is Willie. Meet Felix.'

She smiled. I smiled. She inclined her head, and with a hand under each breast knelt on the edge of the stage. Her knees touched mine while she unhooked the clasp at each hip, silver powder drizzling with the slide of silk on skin. She took a comb from her hair, then another, leaning forward to smother my face. The music blasted, the hair lifted like a curtain and she posed centre stage while the drapes hissed shut.

Fat Man fumbled for a cigarette. 'Like it?'

'I like it.' I dusted silver off my knees and set her bra on the edge of the stage. 'Where'd you get it?'

'It's a new act.' That was the choir-boy. 'We're just getting it right.'

'Looked right to me.'

The girl pushed through the curtain, hair tumbling over a white beach-robe. The choir-boy skipped on to the stage and pushed the drapes back. His hair was combed too careful.

'Marvellous, darling, marvellous.'

She took a packet of Dunhill from her pocket, watching the choir-boy like he'd crawled up from the bottom of the garden.

'One or two little things, though, sweetie, teeny little things, but we must get them right please. For instance when you go into this movement . . .' he swayed skinny hips, 'don't forget the little extra on the fourth beat, one two three and . . .'

The bird rested her elbow on her hand and blew a sabre of smoke.

Fat Man breathed. 'How much?'

'One-sixty a bottle.' I sat up. 'I got twenty dozen.'

'At one-sixty you will not get a taker, you know that, don't you?' He puffed his cheeks like a pudding. 'It is too big a quantity, twenty dozen for one-sixty.'

I laughed. 'Yeah? I got another forty dozen already spoken for at the same price. This is just the tail end.'

'Terrific, darling.' The choir-boy was dribbling all over the bird. He turned to Fat Man. 'Do you want to add anything?'

Fat Man struggled in his seat. 'Just get here on time. None of your pissing about, you are not Sarah Bernhardt, right?' The girl stubbed her fag and turned her back.

'Eleven-fifteen, dear. Take care.' The choir-boy put a hand on her arse.

She wheeled, hair flairing like a cape. 'Leave your hands under your raincoat where they belong, you inadequate neuter.' Like a cut-glass pike. The choir-boy gaped after her.

Fat Man sighed. 'Colin.' The choir-boy started to explain. 'Piss off.'

Colin melted.

'The tail end,' I said.

'I believe you. But you are not getting one-sixty.' I sighed.

'In the words of the guru, don't spit in the custard, you might get prunes for afters. Don't you see this could be the start of a long and fruitful association between our respective organizations? Or don't you care?'

'One-fifteen.'

'One-fifty. D'you want it or not?'

'At that price, no.'

I started to get up. 'Talking to you's like spreading bricks on your toast. I'll come back when the Guv'nor's here, eh?'

His nasty little eyes flashed red. 'I make my own decisions.'

'Congratulations.' I pushed down the row. 'Nice to have an understanding Guv'nor. I'll tell him when I meet him.'

'Siddown.'

I hoisted the carton under my arm. 'Mind how you go.'

'One-twenty-five.'

'One-forty.'

He blew his nose. 'Newcastle, eh?' He lifted the carton out of my hands. 'When can you deliver?'

'When you get the bread.' I glanced about. 'Don't suppose you carry much of a float here.'

'We got it.'

'Good.' I perched on the stage. 'You can have it now then.'

'Now?'

'D'you wannit or not?'

He tried twice to get up. 'How much did we say?'

'One bloody forty.'

'Got transport?'

'Van.'

'Right.' He waded up the aisle. 'There's a yard out the back. Bring it round.'

I fetched the Bedford and found a service lane that ran parallel to the High Road behind the casino. Nothing so grand at the back. A spade held the gates open, showing a tarmac yard and a pile of dustbins down one side, not a sniff of castles in Spain, just a dirty brick wall with carsie windows looking into the yard and a flight of rickety steps leading to the back door. Fat Man stood on the landing. I parked the Bedford and unlocked the doors.

'Gino.' Fat Man leaned into the doorway. 'Come and give Golly a hand.'

A young geezer in tight trousers and bushy sideburns clattered down the steps. He and Golly unloaded while Fat Man and me stood about.

'In the store,' he told them. I followed. We walked down a passage smelling of booze and into a store piled with crates and empty bottles. I looked around.

'Getting ready for the Brownies' Jamboree, then?' Fat Man shifted a crate. 'The more they drink the more they spend on the tables.' He was panting. 'Over there, son.'

When Gino and Golly finished up Fat Man rolled a piggy eye at me. 'Why are the cartons open?'

I squinted. 'Wouldn't you?'

'How many?' He asked Gino.

'Nineteen.'

'Er, one inside the theatre,' I reminded him.

He checked the bottles in each carton. 'I don't like price tabs. What did you do? Smash and grab a Waitrose or what?' His chins shook.

'Your problem.' I yawned. 'Tabs won't cost nothing.'

'Gino. Fetch me a glass.' Fat Man's eyes almost disappeared with the excitement of it all. 'Fancy a jar, Willie?'

'You go ahead.' I lit a cigar.

Gino came back with a glass and Fat Man selected a bottle from the furthest carton. He snapped the seal like paper, dropped two fingers in his tumbler, cupped his hands and sniffed with his eyes shut.

'Is the hooch to Sir's taste?' I asked. 'Or maybe Sir fancies a soupçon of tonic? Give it that touch of je ne sais quoi?'

His eyes welled open and he swallowed the rest like water. 'Right.' He tossed the glass to Golly. Fat Man was starting to relax and I reckoned it was time to forge lifelong friendships.

'Lost two grand in one night coupla months back.' I watched him pull a wad from his hip pocket. 'Roulette.'

'Where was that, then?' He must've wished it was here.
'Vegas.'
'Fit-up. Specially there, according to what I've heard.'
'Go on.'
'Three hundred and thirty-six.' He counted the notes into my palm. 'OK?'
I tucked it away. 'Didn't put me off, though.'
'Play often, do you?'
I shrugged. 'When I'm flush. Win some, lose some.' I blew a smoke-ring. 'Run a straight place here, do you?'
He tried to look hurt. 'Why don't you drop by one night?'
'Why don't I?'
'Five quid limit. You can't go far wrong.' He waved me to the door. 'Small stakes, fast turnover. Salesmen from Sidcup, know what I mean?'
I looked doubtful. 'Not much excitement?'
'We pay our debts.' I squeezed past him in the passage. 'And collect them.'
I backed the van into the service lane while he stood like a mound of dumplings.
'I'll stop by some time.'
'See you.'
On a dark night you'd mistake his hand for a pillow.

Even Streatham air tastes good with three and a half ton in your pocket and a plan to treble it.

Six

The sun was fresh and made you think of summer. I couldn't see a spot for the Bedford in Charlotte Street so I rolled it up to Fitzroy Square and left it where the motor-merchants shine Old Bill's boots with readies. Then I strolled down to Loftus on the corner of Great Percy Street.

Loftus sells the makings to home-brewers, not my bag since anything I can do Watneys do better, but then home-brewers aren't the only berks to blind themselves with their own brilliance. I'd noticed some tubes in the window when passing a couple of days previous and I was developing a professional interest in tubes due to my preoccupation with forty dozen bottles of a certain distillation what had fallen off a lorry not a million miles from Royal College Street last Wednesday week. Loftus sports an old-fashioned counter and the floor sniffs of hops and grapejuice, the shelves being draped with enough tubing to strangle the League Division Four and still leave some for slingshots. The rubber stuff was cut in lengths of five feet, designed for use with pipettes and syphons. I chose twelve lengths, maybe three-sixteenths diameter, and laid them on the counter. An old bird counted them.

'Listen,' I said, 'I want something similar only with twelve lengths connected to one outlet. Know what I mean?'

'Pig's teat.'

'Oh.'

'You won't get a twelve-branch. Six is the biggest.'

'Let's have a look.'

She held up a hose showing six connections. I paid and she gave me a carrier-bag for free.

I drove towards Camden Town and ran into a jam at Mornington Crescent so I dropped the Bedford behind the Electricity Board and walked into the High Street. The cause of the jam was a mob of micks drinking tea down a hole in the road, waiting for the four-thirty pay-off when the Nigels started trying to get home to Hampstead. There's a hardware shop on the East side of the street next to a discount carpet store so I skipped in there and asked for a centre-punch. The assistant laid out a few and I chose one by Vitrex, size 2C. Then I bought a hammer.

Kalinikou was sorting through the scrap with a feller in overalls when I got to the yard and he waved me past without speaking. I sat in the office pulling faces at the dog till Kalinikou stepped inside brushing the rust off his hands.

'So. We have the buyer?'

I nodded and he went into one of those Greek dances, snapping fingers like salami till the dog howled.

'How much?'

'Quid a bottle. At twenty dozen you're a rich Greek.' He held out a hand. 'Not so fast.' I picked the bracelet out of my pocket. 'Remember? You owe me sixty quid.'

His fingers left marks on his shirt pocket when he pulled out the roll. 'What we said for the bracelet? Two-fifty?'

'Three hundred.' I passed a hand over my face. 'Two-forty I've got. You owe me sixty.'

He winded me with a slap and I took off my jacket to see if he'd left marks on the velvet.

'Harry. You have no humour. Here, I give you.' He smacked a wad into my palm. I gave him the bracelet and he danced some more, eyes closed, holding the sparklers to his cheek.

'And you can stop poncing about. There's work to do. Open the back.'

He unlocked. 'What is this in the paper bag?'

'Fifteen miles of rubber tube.' I followed him into the back room. 'Now get on the blower to your mate, the one you're selling to. Will he take delivery in jerry-cans?'

Kalinikou frowned. 'He take in teapots if I say. He trusts me. Why?'

'Wanna get rich? Don't ask questions. Just tell him he's getting delivery in six-gallon jerry-cans, OK?'

'What . . . ?'

'And when you've done that buy some jerry-cans in the High Street, six-gallon type.'

'Harry. You want I go bust, huh? They are maybe two pounds fifty each.'

'So I'll split the cost with you.' I snatched his pen from his shirt and scratched sums in the condensation on the wall. 'We'll need . . . fourteen of them.'

'What . . . ?'

'Just do it.' I pushed him out.

I hung up my jacket and laid punch, tubes, hammer and tabs on the floor, listening to Kalinikou having a bunny next door. Then I bust a carton and chose a bottle, casting about for a suitable surface. There was a plank in the corner. I dusted off the cobwebs, stood the bottle on the wood and set the punch dead centre of the cap. A whack with the hammer. The punch left a neat hole. I cleared the newspapers off the shelf over the sink and found an enamel jug under the draining-board that looked like Kalinikou's coffee-boiler. It took a bit of cleaning and I finished up with brown stains all over my best handkerchief. Kalinikou opened the door.

'He says all right . . .'

'Watch.' I pushed a tube through the hole in the bottle-cap till it touched bottom and set the whole thing on the shelf over the sink. Holding the jug in one hand I sucked on the end of the tube and dropped it in the jug as the vodka touched my tongue. I spat in the sink. 'Time it.' The bottle emptied into the jug.

'One minute.'

The tap fitted the six-branch hose. I got the empty vodka bottle off the shelf and shoved one of the branches through the hole in the cap, leaving the rest dangling in the sink. The bottle filled with water in twenty seconds. I scribbled £3.50 on one of the Blick stickers, yanked the tube out of the bottle and covered the hole with the vinyl tab, then, carefully, the price tab. I held the bottle upside down.

'Bingo.'

Kalinikou threw his hairy arms round my neck and filed my cheek with his jaw. 'Harry!'

'Get off.' He was hopping with excitement, which I put down to his upbringing. 'If you don't get those cans none of us'll have our dinners tonight.'

He went out jabbering, then stuck his head round the door again. 'My friend. The Cretan . . .'

'What about him?'

'He says . . . for vodka in tin cans he pays only ninety pee one bottle.'

'Bloody crook.' I thought. 'Still, I'll sell for round the eighty mark in South London, so you could say you were grossing one-seventy a shot. Like it?'

Kalinikou rolled his eyes and left.

I lit a cigar and picked up the punch. By the time I heard Kalinikou getting the cans off the Bedford I'd punched nearly fifty caps.

We stored the cans in the office and locked the yard gates. I passed the punch to Kalinikou. 'I'll work the pumps for a bit.' He chose a bottle, watching the cap like it was the Evil Eye come to stick the horrors on wayward Greeks. 'No scratches, right? Every cap you scratch means eighty pence down the sluice and forty of it's yours.' I thought about Fat Man. 'I'll be strapped to a stone in the river so it won't bother me. And no bits in the water either. We ditch every bottle that isn't perfect.' I fetched a jerry-can from the office and set twelve punched bottles on the draining-board, pushing a tube into each before lifting them to the shelf. 'Cheers.' By the time I sucked on the twelfth tube the first three bottles were empty. 'Christ.' I rinsed my mouth under the tap. 'Don't swallow any.' I set the empties back in their carton and reached for the next dozen. Each can held thirty-six bottles.

There were times during that afternoon when I did some abstract thinking like what are we all here for but every time a bottle emptied the register said one pound so I tried to stop philosophising and think of banks. Kalinikou nipped out now and then for bits of Greek sausage but I never stopped except to smoke. During the evening my head got so jokey I had to quit. The room was lurching like a cat-house on a Friday night. I told Kalinikou to take over the pumps while I had a kip in the office. He woke me at half-eleven.

'All done.'

His eyes were rimmed mauve and he swayed soft as a palm by the sea. The bottles were empty and we'd filled thirteen and a quarter cans. There were seven rejects against the wall. I held Kalinikou vertical and helped him into his anorak.

'Let's eat.'

We staggered to the nearest Greek caff. Kalinikou knew the gaffer and there was lots of shouting and slapping of backs but they must've thought he was going down with cholera or something because he just wasn't his normal self. In fact he was pissed stupid. He barely touched his dinner, watching while I soldiered through the lamb and beans, but he'd started to rabbit again after his third muddy coffee. When we left there was more yelling and patting of faces. The cold air rinsed my brain on the way back.

Inside the shop I had a look at the bottles while Kalinikou got his head down on the office table. I ditched another eight. Then, lining them six at a time, I connected the hose to the tap, wrapped a pair of towels round the labels, and let them fill with water. A few got wet in spite of the towels and I set them with others against the wall. By four o'clock it was done. Two hundred and four bottles of water, twenty-five rejects and another eleven I'd left empty. I took the price-tabs into the office, cleared a space near Kalinikou's head and filled them in without peeling them off. I got writer's cramp and I had a headache. The sun was shining when I woke Kalinikou.

'Oy. Stickers.'

He looked horrible. 'Why you left those?' He pointed to

the lines of empties.

'Insurance.'

We did each crate together, first the vinyl disc then the paper tab. At half-seven I stretched.

'That's it. I'm going home. See you about one.' Kalinikou yawned like the MGM lion. His tongue was yellow. I drove the 1300 back to the gaff and crashed into kip just as the citizens were untangling the sheets.

At twelve I sorted my change and called the Alhambra from the phone in the hall.

'Lemme speak to the Fat Man.'

'Hang about.'

I heard the phone bounce as Fat Man approached. He made a noise like a compressor.

'Yeah?'

'Willie.' I kept the words short like it was urgent. 'You remember me from yesterday.'

'Who?'

'Willie. I brought the Smirnoff. Look, you want more of the same?'

I heard him blow his nose. 'Wassermadder, Willie?' His voice was soft. 'Thought you said the rest was spoken for?'

'So it is. I've just come by a drop more, that's all.'

'How much more?'

'Well . . . how much d'you want?'

'How much are you offering?'

I stammered. 'I could do you, er, thirty-forty dozen.' The last words tripped over themselves.

Fat Man laughed nasty. 'That is a familiar figure, Willie boy. But then I might have got you confused with somebody else. They are always round here flogging something, you know.'

'Can you use the extra?'

His voice hardened. 'Not at your prices I can't.'

'One-thirty?'

'It's a buyer's market, mate. One-fifteen and count yourself lucky.' I waited. 'Well?'

I choked. 'OK. I'll be down about five. Forty dozen. Get the bread ready.'

Then I fell on the bed and laughed.

Kalinikou was waiting in the yard, anorak zipped up tight.

'How's Adonis this morning, then?'

'No more.' He looked sick.

I lifted the keys out of his fingers. 'Never mind. Tomorrow you can take your winnings and sun yourself down at Clacton.'

'Clacton shit.'

We checked the bottles in the back room and I counted thirty-six empties including the rejects.

'Now I want eleven bottles to each carton.'

While Kalinikou sorted I set aside four cartons with twelve bottles each. That meant the load was thirty-six bottles short which was a lot of boodle if you worried about that sort of thing. I marked each of the four full cartons near the bottom corner with Kalinikou's pen. When we loaded the van I made sure I knew where they were. Kalinikou let me out of the yard at half-three.

'I'd flog that stuff in the jerry-cans if I was you,' I told him.

His shoulders drooped. 'No van.'

'See you later. Think of Clacton.'

Gino was waiting at the back of the Alhambra. I backed up near the door and climbed out spinning the keys on my finger. Golly came out with Fat Man already dressed for the evening's action.

'Well well.'

'Got the gelt?'

'All in good time.'

Gino and Golly started off-loading while Fat Man watched, his tongue playing over lips thick as tyres. 'Got a still down the garden, have you, Willie?'

I checked my watch. 'I'm in a hurry. You'll need more than two blokes.'

Fat Man shrugged. 'All go, isn't it?'

'D'you mind?' I lifted two marked crates.

'Help yourself.'

When we'd finished you could hardly move inside the store. The marked cartons were on top of the pile.

Fat Man leaned on the door as I dusted my hands. He was picking his teeth with a match. 'Fancy a snort?'

My palms pricked. 'The readies first.'

'Some people have got no manners.' He leered, match stuck in his front teeth. 'Gino. Get the brown envelope off of my desk.' He waddled into the store, hands behind his back. 'Let's have a look, then.'

Golly took a carton off the top and bust it open. 'OK.' Fat Man hummed a tune. 'You don't mind, do you, love?' He held a bottle up to the light.

I pushed in front, tearing the lid off the carton next to his. 'Happy?'

Fat Man peered into the carton as Gino came back with an envelope. He passed it through the doorway. Fat Man spat out the match.

'There you go.' He tossed the envelope.

I raised a finger in salute and turned to the door, counting as I went. I was in the passage when Fat Man called.

'Willie.'

He said it soft but Golly was already beside me, fingers tight on my arm. Back in the store Fat Man was staring at a carton of eleven bottles.

'Bet you used to get the stick at school, Willie.' He clucked his tongue. 'Not much cop at sums, are you?' He took the envelope from my fingers. 'Now if you will just stop there I shall have the lads make a count in case you made any more mistakes. I mean, fair's fair, eh?' He turned to Gino. 'Go and fetch Percy.'

The bastards opened every case.

After twenty minutes Fat Man leaned a shoulder against the architrave and mopped his bald patch.

'Tell you what I shall do. I reckon there is a good forty bottles missing.' He shook his head. 'Nasty. Bad mistake.' The fat creased round his mouth. 'But we like you. Don't we, boys?' Percy was making little noises in his throat. 'Lock the door, Perce.'

Percy pushed the others into the passage. There wasn't enough air for three of us in the store. Fat Man hummed.

'Now, I am not going to ask Percy to do the usual.' I could feel Percy quivering like wire. 'No. Nasty business. Mucks up my nice clean floors. No, I shall just take compensation out of your pay-packet. Let me see . . . there is near . . . five and a half ton here. Now, if I was not so narked I would just knock off, say, fifty nicker, wouldn't I?' His fingers gripped my hair, bending me till I faced the floor. 'But I will not tell a lie, Willie. I *am* narked. No. I am hurt. I am very very hurt.'

I didn't see his knee coming but suddenly I was on my hands staring dumb at my reflection in his toe-caps wondering who'd dropped the shutter on my mind. He moved back while I clawed upright.

'I will tell you what I am going to do. Because me and the boys have taken a shine to you I shall be happy to forget your little mistakes. I shall simply deduct justifiable compensation for all the aggro you've caused us. Then I am going to let you go. How much do you reckon you owe me?' I mumbled into my handkerchief. 'Can't hear you. I shall tell you. Another fifty quid. Fair's fair, eh? Sort of poetic justice?' He stuffed the envelope into my jacket pocket. 'There's four-fifty.' Percy unlocked the door and Fat Man shoved me into the passage. 'That was a pleasure.' Golly and Gino were grinning. 'Come again. Any time.' I could hear them laughing from the yard.

I stopped at a public carsie in the Brixton Road to clean myself up and count the quiddies. Four and a half ton. For nothing. Well, almost nothing. What was a face like mashed potato compared to that kind of gelt?

Seven

It was near half-eight when I got to Charlotte Street, time for the trendies to swop suits for jeans and join the riot in the Anemos. The street was lit and the Stags were nudging the kerb, spilling birds in striped socks and blokes who argued the cost of fuel-injection. Bishop was still minding the shop, counting the take behind drawn blinds. My face felt like El Alamein the morning after, and the climb to the attic played tunes on my tendons. It was parky so I lit the fire and mixed a cup of Nescafé. Then I carried the cup and a cigar to the phone.

'Dennis?'

'Harry. What happened?'

'Nothing much.' I drew on the cigar. 'Got my nose splashed by a pudding. Apart from that it was all comedy.'

'How much?'

'Seventy pence a bottle.'

He sighed. 'I thought it would be more.'

'So did I sweetheart.' I spoke through my teeth. 'But like I say I got a couple of medals too so it wasn't a flop.'

'Sorry Harry.'

'Love you too. Anyway, three and a half ton for forty cartons of MWB 1977 isn't that ugly, is it?' He laughed. 'Look, I'm buggered. See you in the morning, all right?'

'OK. What time?'

'I gotta call to make first. Say about twelve unless you want the van before.'

'No. I make the delivery in the afternoon.'

'And listen. I might just be dangling another little trinket so get your gelt ready.'

I spent a couple or three hours winding down for kip. First a bath. The water was warmed by an Ascot that used to swallow pennies, since got above itself with a thirst for shillings. I lay back with the bubbles popping on my chin and *Sporting Life* an inch above the water, trying to suss what was carving the turf at Epsom and Newmarket these days. Then I took a gander at my boat in the mirror. Kiddies do not actually scream at the sight of me but at the same time I can't afford to lose points, and a purple nose was not going to boost my chances. Course, my countenance might be expected to improve in more salubrious environs, I mean Noël Coward furniture and bog-brown walls would rumple Robert Redford, but suppose Harry Saltzman called tomorrow?

If I forget thee O Fat Man.

Crab must've been nicked. I won't say the thought prompted suicide but Crab was a presence you got used to, like a mouse in the kitchen, and I wasn't tickled by the idea of anyone I knew chewing porridge. I just hoped the filth didn't lean too heavy because Crab was not one to bite back whatever the state of his gums. But more important, he was my only connection with this Newcastle mob and I had to decide whether to plug in and find them or drop the idea. Funny. I'd come three thousand miles on a wink and a nudge without a cuss for the prospects. Maybe the truth was it had been coming on Smoke-time again whatever the offer. It was deep thoughts like that that finally pitched me into the bottomless kip.

Shiv Lacey lived in Dartmouth Road which I reckoned was built about nineteen-oh-nothing and looked it, a mile or so of semis playing castles behind a row of skinny trees. You can't live there without wheels on account of one end being a mile from the tube and the other two miles from the buses. The first hustler to hire scooters both ends will clean up.

It was mild and quiet at the East end, a sort of background for the action half-way down. A couple of fire-engines, a fuzz-wagon and a mob like flies round a bear's nose. I stopped the Bedford two blocks away, backed into a space and strolled like I was looking at the time of day. Lacey's gaff looked like the White House after the English stopped by for a smoke. The walls were standing and the roof was in its usual place but the windows were holes blackened at the edges. Water was running down the brickwork, along the path and over the pavement to the gutter, hoses knotted everywhere you looked. The Law stood about bending knees and nattering to firemen's helmets. I pushed at the edge of the crowd. Glass crunched underfoot and two firemen carried out what was left of a couch and chucked it in the front garden. Threads of smoke curled and split in the breeze.

'What happened?' I nudged the bloke next to me.

He looked amazed. 'Fire.'

'Anybody hurt?'

A hen wrapped in a dressing gown pinched a fag to her lips. 'She's gone you know, oh yes. Such a nice person. Lovely to talk to. She's gone.' She puffed. 'Him too, by the look of him when they carried him out. Not long in this world I'd say. By the look of him.'

'When?'

'Middle of the night. Crying shame. Such a nice person.'

'Where'd they take him?'

'Royal Free, they usually go.'

I gunned the van down the Kilburn High Road, round West End Lane and up to the Finchley Road. Two more turns took me into wooden bead country where kids go comprehensive by day and play Chopin by night. Down Rosslyn Hill and into Pond Street with the hospital hanging its bulk over the manor. I parked outside the Roebuck and skipped across the forecourt into Reception.

'Lacey. Came in this morning. I gotta see him.'

The bloke leaned his elbows on the desk. 'Relative, sir?'

'Brother.'

He did something with the cards on the wall. 'Smithson Ward. Fourth floor. He came out of surgery at six.'

The Royal Free isn't like hospitals when I last stopped over. The wards are more like little alcoves carrying four or six beds, four alcoves to a ward with a nurse sitting at a desk watching comings and goings.

'Lacey?'

She pointed. 'Over there. But I don't think . . .'

'I'm his brother.' Lacey was awake, at least I thought he was. The right side of his face was bound like a turban slipping sideways. His left cheek was cut, treated with yellow antiseptic, and his eye glittered like a diamond in your palm, unblinking.

'Shiv?'

'They done it. They bloody went and done it.'

I pulled up a chair and made a business of sitting down.

'Bearing up, then? That's the way. You won't be in here long, mate.'

'Bastards.'

'Listen. I know you're not up to business right now and I don't wanna bother you so I'll try and keep it short, right? The ruby, Shiv. Have you got the ruby?'

'You tell them . . .' his eye rolled, 'tell them . . .'

'Shiv, listen to me.' I leaned closer. 'Where'd you put the sparkler? You can tell me. I got the loot, you see.' I was starting to wish I hadn't come. 'How much did we say? Shiv? How much d'you want? I can go a bit over the asking price, maybe . . .'

Sweat glossed his cheeks. 'Cora. Bastards . . .'

'Look, mate, I can see you're not in the mood for talking shop but please, you gotta try. Have you sold it yet?'

'She done nothing. When you see them . . .'

'Who, Shiv?' I didn't want to know. 'Why'd they do it?'

'. . . tell . . . tell them . . .'

'Shiv.' I almost touched him. 'The sparkler. Try and think. Did you sell the sparkler?'

His eye was like a Dartmoor searchlight. 'They got her.'

'Look, I'm sorry . . .' I stood up.

'. . . tell him I'll . . .'

I backed through the curtains. 'Sorry about the missus. Sorry.'

My gut wasn't straight till I'd sunk three doubles at the Roebuck.

I coasted down the hill thinking about Lacey. Somebody had dropped the axe and it didn't stretch the intellect of Harry G to connect the fire with the sparklers so to speak. I mean that bracelet was trouble, and the route from Lacey to me was that clear I could feel the teeth on my heels already. Time, I thought, to scarper. I had not flown three thousand miles to get my best suit scorched.

The gates on Kalinikou's yard were shut so I didn't bother backing the van up but left it with one wheel on the pavement next to the 1300. The dog stood in the yard, chain dragging through the scrap-iron so I yelled for Kalinikou to tie him down before I lost a leg. He didn't answer. A train rumbled overhead and the dog drooped his ears, chin on his paws. I walked backwards to the door to keep him in sight.

'How do.'

That wasn't Kalinikou. I was three steps from the gate when somebody caught my collar and crashed my shoulder into the wall. A boot kicked my feet outwards as I clutched for the brickwork.

'Legs apart!' Again the boot. I rested on the palm of my left hand, sucking air and fighting for balance. Whoever he was he was busting my arm. 'Mind out, Sunshine, or I'll break your fucking neck.' I believed him. 'Fingers on the wall. Both hands.'

I had no feeling in my right arm but I did what he said, staring at my reflection in an old car bumper on the ground.

'What . . . ?'

'Shut it.' Another voice. From the office. I lifted my eyes to the bloke leaning on the door. Pale and thin, eyes bleached so you could barely see his pupils. He was bald on top and collected his hair on one side, draping it like a shawl over his head, where it separated into strands showing slicks of scalp.

He wore an old-fashioned raincoat cut just above the knee. He squinted through the smoke from the fag between his lips. 'Take a look.' Hands clawed from behind. 'Clean.'

'If you blokes . . .'

'Shut it.' Ash dropped down the pale one's raincoat. 'Get him inside.'

A fist spun me from the shoulder and I looked into a face you could've sold to Bethlehem at Christmas.

'Walk.'

'Watch it.' I tripped. 'This body mightn't look much but it's life and death to some.' I fell into the office. The pale one was sitting at Kalinikou's table, fingers laced behind his head. I massaged my arm. 'Christ you . . .'

'Shut it.' Paleface sat up, elbows on the table. His mouth twitched. 'Flying Squad.' He flashed a card. 'My name is Quist. Detective-Sergeant Quist. Q.U.I.S.T. And whatever else you do between now and Wormwood Scrubs don't you forget it.' He balanced on two legs of the chair. 'So. What's my name?'

It's easy to see how some coppers get themselves molested. I levelled my eyes at his scalp.

'Verily it is quoth, as the yam finds root between the corn, so shall hair on Beachy Head be born. Corinthians Chapter five Verse two. But don't give up . . .' I finished on a gasp, pain reminding me that bogeys came in twos.

'What's his name?'

I faced the other one. 'His name is Detective-Sergeant Quist. Second Class. Spelt C.U. . . . forget it. What do they call you. Yvonne de Carlo?'

Quist pointed. 'That is Detective-Constable Ryan. He hates people who can't remember my name.'

When Ryan stopped curling his lip he looked like a son any mother would've been proud of. 'Let's get him down the factory.' His eyes were hard as a navvy's fist.

Quist let the chair fall straight, pressing the tips of his fingers together. 'All in good time.' He ground his cigarette into the floor and chose another. 'Empty your pockets.' I turned out wallet, handkerchief, keys, notebook, pen, cigars and lighter. 'That's it.'

Quist ran his nicotined nail down the pages of the notebook. 'Check.'

Ryan shoved. The bulge in my back pocket was obvious. He dropped the bankroll on the table and Quist picked it up.

'My. That's a lot of money.' He raised his eyes. 'How'd you come by this?'

'Selling kisses in a fairground.'

Quist was counting the notes. 'Funny how the jokers lose their sense of humour after a drop of bird, isn't it, Constable Ryan?'

Ryan smirked. 'Isn't it?'

'Where'd you get it?'

'Gee-gees.' I put my hands on my hips. 'Don't tell me the old Whip-and-Rod are into horse flesh too?'

'What race?'

I thought of *Sporting Life*. 'Four-thirty at Newmarket last Saturday.'

'Horse?'

'Clear Sky.'

Quist wiped a drop of spit off his mouth. 'Nearly nine hundred pounds.' He sucked his teeth. 'What bookie?'

'Tote.'

'What's your name?'

'My name?'

'I suppose your mother never gave you one?'

'No.'

'No what?'

'No she never.'

'What's your name?' Quist unbuttoned his raincoat and slipped his hands into his trouser pockets. His shirt was nylon, creased like a Naafi tea-towel. 'I'll tell you then. Harry Grant.'

I swallowed. 'We've all been introduced then.'

'Harry Grant.' Quist stood up, hitching his belt round a waist too thick for his build. 'I'll tell you a story. You came here with a set of sparklers and flogged them to the Greek.' There were stains on his teeth. 'Like it so far?'

'Sparklers?' I turned to Ryan. 'What's he on about? What

sparklers?'

'These sparklers.' The bracelet twinkled on Quist's fingers.

I creased my forehead. 'Nice, aren't they?'

'Yours?'

'Sorry.'

A vein throbbed in Quist's temple. 'Let me rephrase that. I know they're not yours. What I mean is did you flog them to the Greek?'

'No I never. Can I go home now please?'

Quist perched on the edge of the table twirling the bracelet. 'Where'd you get them, Harry?'

'Get bloody what?'

He waited while a train passed. 'We've had this cess-pit watched for a couple of weeks. Seen you coming and going. When we picked up the Greek we asked him about the sparklers, see, and he said you sold them to him. Straight up.' He walked round the table, rolling his fag from one side of his mouth to the other. 'And if you're making plans for the Greek forget it. He'll be an old man when he gets out. So will you.'

It wasn't likely Kalinikou had grassed but even if he had it was his word against mine. If I stayed cool they couldn't make it stick.

'Look.' I was wearing my reasonable face. 'I just got back from the States . . .'

'We know.'

'. . . and I'm still suffering from jet-lag. I mean, I just haven't had time for sparklers and stuff even if I was a member of the criminal classes which I do assure you I will take pains to prove I am not. No way. I just came to see the Greek on account of him being an old mate from Piraeus.' I sighed. 'And what do I get for my thoughtfulness? Police brutality. Get off, will you?'

'Regular amnesiac, aren't you?' Quist was developing a pink spot on each cheek. 'Or maybe you sleep-walk. Don't kid the coppers, old son. You been seen hanging about this manor for the past four days. And the Greek speaks English you know.'

'What did you do? Whip the soles of his feet? People will

say anything under duress you know. And to think citizens like me pay the wages of the likes of you. Straight up, it's a national scandal.'

'Citizens like you pay bugger-all,' said Ryan. 'Let's have a look at the back room.'

He pushed me through. The jerry-cans were stacked neat for loading.

'Suppose you know nothing about this either?' He unscrewed a cap and tasted his finger. 'Vodka.'

'You used to beat up Greeks until you discovered Smirnoff.' I shrugged. 'How would I know?'

'Yours?' He screwed the cap tight.

'Wish it was.'

Quist stood near the door, buttoning his raincoat.

'Come on. We've got enough. And we've hung so much on the Greek he'll ask for the booze TIC. Let's get this feller down the factory and do it proper.'

Ryan opened a plastic bag and dropped my gear in. Quist locked the back room and lead me into the yard, White Fang was stretched mournful by the gates.

'What'd you do to the dog?' I watched Ryan lock up. 'Put glass in his porridge?'

Quist let his mouth twitch. 'Funny you should mention porridge.'

He sat close to me in the back of the Escort. His breath smelled. Bad.

Eight

The Edgware Road runs from Marble Arch to the North Circular, a distance of, I don't know, maybe five or six miles. It changes names along the way, Maida Vale, Kilburn High Road and Shoot-Up Hill whatever that might mean, and being one of the arterial routes North it carries heavy traffic. There used to be bother at the junction with the Marylebone Road till they built the flyover, which nowadays marks the boundary of the West End as surely as a gate. Class begins at Marble Arch and comes full stop at the London Metropole. North of that it's rubbish all the way apart from a short stretch along Maida Vale. And the nick squats on the North edge of the flyover opposite the Metropole.

Ryan slid the Escort into the car park and let us out of the back. They marched me up the front steps and I came out in a sweat at the smell. The building was new, glossy in the way you'd expect of Old Bill, which is to say marble showing the truth at the edges. The charge desk stretched the length of the lobby like an airstrip and I've never seen so many bogeys in one place. Ryan held my arm while Quist had a natter with the desk sergeant, glancing at me while I inspected the Marks and Sparks decor. Then Quist took charge.

'Better call Collinson. Ask him what action. I'll mind our friend here.' He led me down a grey and blue corridor. 'There you go Harry. Second door left.' We stood in a small hot room, grey and blue like the corridor, looking square at the underside of the flyover through frosted glass. A table took up most of the space, lined by half a dozen chairs each side.

'Boardroom?'

'Sit down.' Quist shut the door and hung his raincoat on a hook. I sat next to a typewriter while he moved the chairs and eased in opposite with his back to the window. He took out a notebook and ran a metal comb through the strands of his hair. 'Where'd you get it?'

'Get what?'

He spread the contents of the plastic bag on the table-top and lifted my bankroll on the end of a pencil.

'Don't come the malarky, son, or I'll make you hate the day you were born. Where'd you get it?'

'Dunno what you're driving at.'

Quist was writing. 'The bracelet. Where'd you get it?' His cheek twitched.

'Never seen it before today so help me.'

He didn't look up. 'Who gave you the bracelet?'

'Nobody gave me anything. I told you, I just got back from New York . . .'

'And you're still suffering jet-lag.'

'Right.'

'Harry.' Quist dropped his notebook and lit a fag. 'You can do better than this.' He found a stained tin-lid and tapped his cigarette on the rim. 'How about something really good, you know, something to give the Super a bloody good laugh? Eh?'

'Sod the Super.' His smoke hung over the table. 'Write that down.'

Quist leaned until the back of his chair fitted into a scar in the plasterwork under the sill. I could see his jaw-muscles working.

'I know more about you than you think for. Bear that in mind. Now if you don't co-operate I am going to make life so bloody unbearable for you you'll beg permission to cut your own throat.' He licked his lips. 'Why don't you just come through? You'll feel a lot better.'

'I feel fine.'

'Not for long, Petal. My bloody oath. Tell me who flogged it to you.'

'Flogged what?'

'The bracelet.'

'Nobody.'

'That's not what the Greek says.'

'Yeah well, he's a foreigner, isn't he? You better not pay attention. Biggest liars in the world, Greeks.'

'He says you dropped by one morning waving this bracelet and asked him to buy it. What d'you say to that?'

I yawned. 'What d'you want me to say?'

'Yes or no.'

'No.'

'Poor old Greek.' Quist's face reminded me of a quarter-moon except it was paler. 'He'll be doing bird for years.' He studied the wet end of his fag. 'Course there's no need for you to go the same way. Not so long, anyway.' He shrugged. 'You won't find the beak ungrateful for a drop of straight talk. I'll put in a word for you.'

'I won't find no beak, period.' I leaned across the table. 'You got no evidence, Quist.' I stood, scraping my chair across the parquet. 'I'll call my solicitor now if you don't mind.'

'Sit.' I sat. 'You're not under arrest yet, old son.' He licked his mouth again. 'You're free to go anytime. Legally.'

'In that case . . .'

'Unless I charge you.' He sucked at his fag. 'We don't like fences, Harry. Nasty people. Deserve all they get.'

Ryan came in and slopped a paper cup on the table.

'Drop of oil for your gizzard, Wal.' He glanced at me. 'He giving you bother?'

Quist flicked pale eyes over the paper rim. 'Harry and me see eye to eye. What did Collinson say?'

'It's not as simple as we thought. When you're ready take him down to Hamilton's office. Collinson'll be there in half an hour.'

I pointed at the cup. 'Where's mine?'

'Chirpy chappie, isn't he?' Ryan's mouth twisted. 'He'll want his nice sparklers back next.'

'He won't.' Quist set down his cup.

'Want me to stay?'

Quist shook his head. 'Mister Grant and me've got a few things to talk over yet, haven't we, Petal?'

'Talk to my solicitor.'

Ryan snorted. 'Bloody hell.' He turned at the door. 'Call me when you're ready.' The partition shook behind him.

Quist cradled his cup in his hands. 'Wanted a cuppa did you, Harry?' I stared past him at the window. 'He's thoughtless, that Ryan. No manners. I'm always telling him about it. But he's young yet so I expect he'll learn.' He sipped. 'When did you say you got back?'

'Five or six days ago.'

'How long did you say you were away?'

'I didn't.'

'How long were you away?'

It's not funny carrying Old Bill on your back and they know it. Isolate you on their own patch and they've got all the time it takes to smash your soul to little bits.

'Nine months.'

'What brought you back?'

'Grey fog. Fog's yellow in New York.'

He rested his chin on his hand, orange fingers stroking one side of his face. 'Takes a lot to bring a feller that distance.'

'If you say.'

His free hand drew circles in his notebook. 'I mean, you wouldn't come all that way for Clear Sky at Newmarket, would you?'

'Why not?'

'What made you go in the first place?' He lit another fag and dropped the match in the tin lid. 'After all, you're a Londoner. Out of your element over there, I should think. Out of your league.'

The needle was close. 'I've never been out of my league in my life.'

Quist's eyes reminded me of a corpse. 'No offence. But I shouldn't have thought there was much scope for back-alley losers like you in New York.'

'Shut it, copper.'

Quist's shoulders roamed the padding of his jacket while he opened his mouth in a silent laugh. 'You don't fool me. You're a dirty little tea-leaf and you'll never be anything else. Every nick in the country's bulging with scum like you. Lice on the dog's back. They oughta top the lot of you and leave room for the men.'

With Quist it was instinct. He was born knowing things others spend their lives learning. And you'd go under unless you fought him with his own weapons.

'Yeah well.' I reached for the cigars. 'We can't all get to be Chief Constable, can we?' I lit up, eyeing the yellow edges of his shirt. 'Takes all types, and thank Christ for that. Some fellers would get really fussed about promotion and such. It's all very well for the bull-artists. They get noticed because they shout loudest. But somebody's got to clean up the mess, right? Somebody's got to tie up the details while they act flash and get promoted.' I shrugged. 'Wouldn't bother me if I was a bogey. But then I'm still young enough to . . .'

'Put that cigar out.' His cheek was twitching again. We sat looking at each other. Then his mouth started to stretch sideways. 'Found Crab?'

I listened to the rumble on the flyover.

'Who?'

'Crab.'

'Crab?' The room was smaller than I'd thought. There wasn't enough air. Quist tucked his notebook into his breast pocket, pinched the end of his fag and laid it careful on the tin.

'Forgotten already? Nine months isn't that long, is it?'

'Crab?' I brightened. 'Used to drive a taxi?'

'That's him.'

'Oh him. No. I haven't seen him. All right is he?' Quist broke a matchstick and started cleaning his fingernails. 'A bit . . . nervous. But all right in himself.' He examined the stains on his fingers. 'Funny you saying you haven't seen him. He went to a lot of bother on your account.'

'How's that then?'

'Getting you home.'

I opened my mouth. 'He never. I just came back.'

'That's funny too.' He worked on his thumbnail. 'Crab and me spent a long while deciding what would get you home fastest. Course, we weren't to know you was just waiting for a chance to drop out of the race anyway.' He lifted his colourless eyes. 'No. I shouldn't be too hard on him.' He dropped the match into the tin and slotted his knuckles together. 'I'd've sent him down for ten years if he hadn't come through. Hobson's choice. What would you have done?' My face was cold. 'I had enough on your skinny friend to turn him inside out at the flick of a fag-end.'

I swallowed. 'Where is he now?'

'Borneo, I should think.'

'Why?'

He selected a cigarette and offered it between thumb and forefinger. 'Don't take it so hard. He didn't have much option.' He lit the fag for me.

'Why?' The nicotine dizzied me.

'I must say you led me a right dance, though. I nearly lost you a couple of times. That's what comes of having too many irons in the fire. Ryan was assigned to the jewel job last week, watching known receivers. When I realized it was you calling on the Greek I had to practically crawl on hands and knees for a transfer to the jewel case. Ties you and me up neat, doesn't it?' He reflected. 'Lucky, that.'

'Why?'

'Why what?'

I was on my feet.

'Why you and me?'

'You'll upset the Super carrying on like that. Sit down.'

'Why?'

'Because,' he sighed, 'I told your pal Crab I'd send him down for ten bloody years if he didn't. That's why.' I fought for breath.

'Why did you want me back? OK, I'm . . . maybe everything you said about me is true. So why bother getting me back?'

Quist dropped ash on the floor. 'That's the way, Harry. Let it all out. I told you you'd feel better.' He gave a sort of giggle. 'Easy once you start, isn't it?'

Easy when you've got a man like a fish on a slab. You're dead unless you think faster than them.

'Still.' I butted my fag in the tin. 'Turned out lucky as it happened. I ought to thank you. Thank you, Sergeant Quist.'

'Come back to a lucky break, Harry?'

'Walked right into it, didn't I?'

'The sparklers?'

I looked shocked. 'Christ no. You don't get me touching that sort of thing. No, this is legit.'

'Worth a bit, is it?'

'You know me. Easy come, easy go. Worth a few bob. Nothing fantastic, but it's a living.'

Quist patted his hair. 'Nothing like that other time. Remember?'

'Quote me.' I spread my hands. 'To which particular time of my life do you allude?'

'Nine or ten months ago, just before you left for America. Somebody offered you twenty grand. Remember?'

I watched the goose-pimples rise on my wrists.

'No.'

'Twenty thousand.' He sighed. 'That was a lot of money. More than you'd ever seen. The trouble was the job.' He nearly smiled. 'Not a hit-man, are you, Harry? I know that. Fiddling gas meters is more your line, right?' My feet were yelling run. 'The way I heard, the deal paid half down and half after, and you saw a way of lifting the first half without getting involved. And ten thousand was more than you'd ever seen too.' He stubbed his cigarette. 'Now, you're a smart lad and I can see you wondering how I know all this, so I'll tell you. One night last year I was called out to the Park Lane Garage. Right bloody mess, that was. Two corpses and one half-dead, all coppers. It was an Irish job. Carson told me the story just before he died. You remember Carson, Harry? The copper that thought he'd hired Cain and got you instead?' A fly buzzed round my head. 'One of my lads got the number of the taxi you left in. Once I'd found your mate Crab, tracking you down was easy.' He paused. 'It was harder finding Cain.'

'He's dead.'

Quist grinned. 'When you think about it, it wasn't really Carson you fooled, was it? You conned a pro. A pro killer. You remember. Tall. Soft voice. Fair hair.'

'I tell you he's bloody dead!'

He shook his head. 'Cain's not dead.'

'You – ?'

'Try and help my friends, don't I?' He folded his arms. 'Don't have to tell you about Cain, do I? I see you remember very well. No mess. He does what he's paid to do. Quietly.' He sighed. 'But that last business . . . very sloppy. Somebody hired *him* to do a job and *you* messed it. So he asked me to speak to you.' A pause. 'He wants his money back.'

I talked round my tongue. 'Haven't got it.'

'That's too bad. Still, he's a reasonable man. He says to tell you the twenty-third, because that's when his commitments take him . . . abroad. That's ten days. A thousand a day. After that . . .' he winked. 'But I can't tell you more than you already know, can I? Think about it, Harry.' He stuck his head into the corridor and called the desk. 'Get Ryan will you?' He lifted his raincoat off the hook. 'Shouldn't be difficult for a smart feller like you. In fact I'm going to make it easy for you.' He dropped my gear into the plastic bag. 'I shan't pin the sparklers on you. Yet. Not for ten days. After that, well, I should think you'll be glad of a couple of years' rest.' He grinned. 'If you're not already resting, so to speak.'

I made a sound.

'Don't thank me.' Quist raised a palm. 'I'm a soft touch, I know.' He put his head on one side. 'Christ you look bad. You want the toilet or something? Clean yourself up, eh? We got a visit to make, you and me. You won't want to be seen like that, will you?'

I followed him to the carsie down the corridor, and he watched me bury my face in a basin of cold water. Ryan met us outside the interview room.

'Ready?' He looked at me. 'Gawd. What happened to him?'

Quist smiled his secret. 'Melting under due process of law.'

'Make it stick?'

'I will.' He patted my shoulder. 'Doesn't matter. We shan't be getting aggro from Mister Grant. Going to be a good lad from now on, aren't you, Harry?' I threw his hand off my shoulder. 'Temper.'

'Got his gear?'

Quist patted his pocket while Ryan laid his palm on my chest. 'Don't worry Squire. We'll straighten you out. We always do.' He adjusted my tie. 'Stone me, you look a mess. Why don't you take more care of yourself? After all, you'll have to look after yourself in the nick, won't you? They don't tolerate sloppy dress there you know, my life.' Quist tossed a wink behind Ryan's back and they marched me out to the Escort.

Nine

The sway of the car swilled my stomach. Shops and crowds unreeled outside, motors gliding close like a slow-motion dance-class. Quist and Ryan spoke shorthand, turning to me for jokes.

'You wanna leave off worrying.' Ryan hummed a pop tune. 'You snuff it at the finish whatever you do so why bust a gut?'

'Comfortable at the Scrubs. Regular meals. Even the screws are kind these days. New directive to the Prisons Department, all screws must contain a minimum fifty-percent humanity.' Quist winked. 'Nothing personal, Harry, I mean, we're just a couple of yobs doing a job. Take Ryan. Just because he's a copper doesn't mean he's got no heart. In actual fact I can assure you Constable Ryan is all heart. Isn't that right, Constable?'

'Dead right, Sergeant.'

Ryan nosed the Escort round the fountains in Trafalgar Square, parked opposite the Whitehall Theatre and pulled a cord that dropped a blind in the back window. It read 'Police'. He let us out of the back and the two of them walked me down the pavement to an entrance sandwiched between the shops. It was narrow and paved with worn stone. We climbed into an old-fashioned trellis lift and stood touching eyeballs while it struggled to the fourth floor. Three unmarked doors led off the lobby, and Ryan opened the one in the middle. It was more like a box-room than an office, six feet wide and lined with files on slatted shelves. A bird sat at a desk painting her nails in the light from the window.

'Good afternoon.' Her eyes flicked at me and stopped on Ryan.

'Hullo, love.' Ryan leaned on the desk. 'Chief about?' The girl screwed the cap on her polish and lifted the phone careful not to smudge her nails.

'Constable Ryan and Mr Quist to see you.' She blushed under Ryan's grin. 'Yes.' She stood, patting her hair. 'Go in please.'

The inner office was badly lit by a window that faced the buildings across Whitehall. The lino on the floor was glossed by years, the smell of polish mixing with the smell of paper, and a heavy desk stood on a square of carpet that might've been blue in a better light. A man stood, silhouetted against the window.

'Quist? Ryan?' He cleared his throat. 'I think you know Inspector Collinson?' I hadn't seen the feller in the corner.

Quist nodded. 'Sir.'

'So this is, er . . .' The bloke behind the desk lowered himself like he needed permission.

'Name of Grant.' Quist put a hand on my back. 'Stand up straight, Harry. This is Mr Hamilton.'

Hamilton half-stood and offered a soft hand. 'How d'you do?' He didn't look at me. 'This is . . . Inspector Collinson . . . Special Branch.' The man in the corner nodded, the lines on his face catching the light from the window. 'Oh . . . please.' Hamilton stuttered. 'Sit down, won't you?' Ryan flipped a chair and pressed me into it. He and Quist formed up behind. 'James . . .' Hamilton's hand fluttered at Collinson, 'perhaps you'd like to . . .'

Collinson filled a pipe, face creased with the weight of decisions. 'I'll not keep you long, Sergeant. Just run through the details, will you?'

Quist cleared his throat and took out his notebook. 'Well, sir,' he held a page to the light, 'during the period 7th to 12th of May, following the business at Mr Hamilton's residence, a detachment from the Flying Squad was assigned to carry out surveillance of known receivers. DC Ryan here was sent to a scrapyard near Kentish Town, run by . . .' he frowned at the page, 'a person known as . . . Demis Kalinikou, an immigrant of Mediterranean origin resident in the UK for fifteen years. The suspect had got five previous convictions for receiving.' He flipped a page. 'At the same time I was observing the movements of the man Grant, who arrived back in this country last week from – '

'Before the theft?'

'No, sir. From America, and who I suspected of intent to commit a felony. Grant has got two convictions, one for obstructing a police officer in the execution of his duty and one for being drunk and disorderly. He visited the scrapyard shortly after his return whereupon I requested urgent transfer to this investigation.' He coughed modestly. 'Owing to the . . . indisposition of the officer in charge I had the good fortune to be appointed in his place. By yesterday the 12th May DC Ryan had got enough evidence to . . . to secure a warrant for the arrest of Kalinikou on a charge of receiving sixty dozen cartons of spirits stolen from a shipment en route to Edinburgh. Once we had him safe we thought we might . . . ask him about the spar – the jewels, sir.' He swallowed. 'The arrest was made at eleven hundred hours this morning as the suspect opened his premises. Among the items in his possession was a diamond bracelet which DC Ryan recognized as the one described in the D14 circulated on 8 May.' He fished in his pocket. 'This.' The bracelet left a scratch on the desk-top. 'DC Ryan then made his report to me. We have reason to suspect that Grant sold the bracelet to Kalinikou.'

Collinson shifted. 'Reason to suspect?'

'Sir.' I felt Quist stiffen. 'With respect, but we've questioned all recent visitors to Kalinikou's yard and none of them's in the sparklers league. None of them passed the bracelet, sir. Take my word for it.'

'Carry on.'

'We therefore apprehended Grant at twelve-thirty today when he called at the yard. He was in possession of eight hundred and ninety-six pounds cash.' Quist lowered the notebook. 'He admits nothing. Yet. Sir.'

Collinson stroked his jaw. 'You've brought Grant's belongings as I asked?' Quist dumped the plastic bag on the desk. 'You intend to charge him?'

'Not yet. Sir. We will.'

Collinson was sifting through my gear. 'Good. Thank you, Sergeant.' He turned to Hamilton.

'Sir?' Quist frowned.

'You may go.'

'Sir?'

'Sergeant Quist.' Collinson got to his feet and moved round the desk. 'The rather . . . unique nature of the theft demands that Special Branch now assume responsibility for all future enquiries. The matter has been cleared with your Superintendent.'

'With respect, sir . . .'

'That's all, Sergeant. Your Super will explain. My department is grateful for your work. Thank you.' He sat down and spoke to Hamilton. 'Have Sergeant Quist shown out, will you, Roger?'

Hamilton lifted the phone. 'Sheila. See Sergeant Quist off the premises please.'

Sheila looked in and stood by the door. Quist tapped me on the shoulder. 'Don't forget, Harry.' He wasn't talking about the sparklers. 'I'll see you around.'

Sheila shut the door behind them.

Collinson and Hamilton sat quiet. Then Collinson lit his pipe.

'Well, Roger. It looks as if you have your chance.'

'I'm . . . grateful.' Hamilton played with a ruler.

'I just hope you're right.' Collinson sighed. 'This could cost you your career. And mine.'

'I know.'

Collinson stood. 'Don't forget. If you need help . . .'

'Thank you, James.' Hamilton took his hand. 'I'm grateful. Very grateful.'

'Best of luck.' Collinson adjusted a felt hat. 'Remember this, Grant. Mr Hamilton has my backing. One hint of obstruction from you and I'll have Sergeant Quist throw the book. Is that clear? Good.' He looked at Hamilton. 'Cheerio, Roger.'

Hamilton saw him to the door, then switched on the light.

He was a slight man, greying hair trimmed round his ears, showing just enough sideburn to be fashionable. He wore a light grey suit that bulged at the knees and a maroon tie with a handkerchief to match. About fifty, I reckoned, carrying it well except for the worry-lines on his forehead. He held his head bowed like begging pardon and wouldn't catch my eye. He fumbled in a drawer, pulled out a packet of Rennies, slipped one in his mouth and smiled at the blotter.

'The police can be . . . unpleasant at times.' His hand rested on his stomach. 'Would you like some tea?' He lifted the phone. 'Sheila? I have a guest for tea today. Oh. And please ask Mr Travis and Mr McLeod if they wouldn't mind coming to my office. Er . . . you'd better ask them if they've had tea.' He had bother setting the phone straight on the cradle. 'We'd best wait until my colleagues are here, if you don't mind, Mr Grant.'

He opened drawers and arranged papers. If a large chunk of my cerebellum hadn't been otherwise engaged I'd have been feeling spare. As it was . . .

Ten days.

A young bloke came in, all man and bounce, the sort that does press-ups before breakfast. His hair was thick, swept in two wings from his forehead, a stray lock tickling his eyebrow. His eyes were blue and his jaw was square, what more can you say? He ought to've been waving a pistol on a lanyard, leading his chaps over the top to posthumous VCs. I looked at his tie. Guards? He grabbed a chair and sat beside me, radiating energy like the sun.

'Mr Grant, er, Michael Travis.' Hamilton unclipped a document while Travis inspected me like I'd tripped him in Harrods. 'I thought you might appreciate this, Michael.' He passed the document over the desk. 'The Minister's report on the Shabani affair.'

Travis set a pair of gold-rimmed specs on his nose and took the report. He smiled. 'Good. Good. Better than you expected?'

'Very much.'

Travis dropped the page on the desk, folded his specs and glanced at his watch. 'Where's the buccaneer?'

'Oh, coming.' Hamilton was anxious and Travis was used to letting him feel it. 'Are you spending the weekend out of Town?'

Travis cocked an eye at the window. 'I thought I might call in at Burnham again. Yes.'

'Good sailing weather?'

'If it holds.' He folded his arms. 'Actually I'd welcome bad weather. Gives one the chance to carry out maintenance.'

'You sailing people.' Hamilton needed friends. 'Sometimes I think you spend more time maintaining than sailing.'

Travis set his left ankle on his right knee. Shoes by Gucci, unless I'd lost touch. 'Part of the fascination.' Come to think of it, that suit must've set him back three ton. You don't get quality like that down the Mile End Road.

The bird came in and set a tray on the desk, careful to avoid the lines of sharpened pencils.

'Thank you, Sheila.' Hamilton stood.

A voice at the door. Travis glanced over his shoulder, eyebrows drawn in distaste. A feller with a crooked smile and a leather jacket leaned on the jamb.

Hamilton lifted the teapot. 'Come in, Gordon.'

The bloke in the doorway wore a fawn roll-neck sweater that bunched into folds round his waist. His hair was wild, a mess of thin grey curls glowing in the light from the outer office. He was rubbing his hands.

'Gordon McLeod. This is Mr Grant.' Hamilton looked into my eyes. 'Milk, Mr Grant?'

I nodded as McLeod tried to bust my fingers. His nails were bitten short.

'Glad to meet ye.'

'Sugar?' Hamilton passed a bowl.

McLeod used the back of his hand to catch the drips from his cup. Travis let his gaze wander the creases in his leather jacket. I swallowed the tea and set the cup on the corner of the desk.

'More?' Hamilton looked at my cup.

'Ta.'

'Perhaps you'd like a . . . biscuit or something?' He scanned the tray and reached for the phone. 'It's not like Sheila to forget.'

'I'm OK.' I didn't want to throw up on his nice blue carpet.

Hamilton cleared his throat. 'Well,' he spoke to the books on the far wall while he reached for his Rennies, 'I'm sure Mr Grant's in no mood to suffer the ramblings of three . . . civil servants, so I'll . . .' he coughed. 'You've probably understood that this is a government department. We're affiliated to the Foreign Office, but . . .' he smiled at Travis who ignored him, 'not respectable enough to occupy offices in the block nearer Westminster. Yet. I'm afraid our work may sound rather boring. We read.' I turned my head. 'Read, Mr Grant. We are economists. We analyze reports from every one of the new African states. That includes newspaper stories, company reports, and, well, material gathered in the field. We are divided into two sections . . . headed by Mr McLeod and Mr Travis.' He patted his stomach. 'More tea?'

Travis couldn't wait. 'We process and feed the information to the FO. It's supposed to give Westminster facts enough to apply pressure when it's needed, the idea being to strengthen Western influence in the emergent states.' Hamilton lifted a finger. 'Mr Travis means economic pressure. We are economists. Not soldiers.'

McLeod poked his fingers in his leather jacket and offered a pack of Gauloises. The ends were ragged and I was careful not to bend them.

'Cheers.'

He spat bits of tobacco. Travis frowned and shifted his chair.

'Nor are we . . . policemen,' said Hamilton. 'We've no interest in your activities unless they affect the Bureau.' His forehead crinkled. 'Now, the bracelet you saw earlier was one of several . . . articles stolen last Saturday night. They were stored in a safe in my house. Another was a chess-set, made by Fabergé and inherited through my wife's family. It was worth many thousands of pounds.' He drew lines on the blotter with his thumb-nail. 'But I'm primarily concerned with the loss of a roll of unprocessed film.'

Ten days.

'Jimmy Collinson has forbidden me to tell you why that film is important. I, er, it was . . . delivered unexpectedly on Saturday night just before my wife and I left for the Guildhall. I locked it in the safe . . .' Travis stirred, 'intending to contact Mr McLeod and Mr Travis in the morning. The burglary was badly timed because my wife was wearing most of the valuable pieces.' He stared at the ceiling. 'Because the film is so important Special Branch asked the CID to report the, um, apprehension of all suspects, and now it looks as if Special Branch will take direct charge.' He lowered his voice. 'Collinson's an old friend. I've persuaded him that this . . . business needs absolute discretion, that we ought to be permitted a chance to recover the film in our own way. I say the film, Mr Grant.' He rubbed his eyes. 'Much as I value the Fabergé the film comes first. And you are the only link Collinson has found.'

I could feel the sunshine at the back of my eyes. 'I didn't nick your jewels.'

Travis looked sour. 'But you know where to start looking.'

'Do I? Anyway, what makes you think the film's still with this chess-set?'

'It may not be.'

'So why should I help?'

Hamilton stared at his fingernails, face heavy with embarrassment. 'Collinson rather thought you would.' He looked to Travis for help.

'What d'you think of Quist?' Travis smiled thin. 'Bit of a hard-liner? I don't think he likes you.'

'I know the type,' said McLeod. 'Ye'll not get a blessing outta him when Collinson gives the nod.'

Oh I'd help all right but not for the reasons they thought. Hamilton's chess-set must be worth a mint.

'This chess-set. What'd you say it was worth?'

Hamilton was sharp. 'I don't see . . .'

'Look, if I'm going to suss the peter-man I've gotta know where to start. So I need to know the weight of the score, right?'

'It's . . . unique.' Hamilton kept his eyes down. 'It was insured for twenty-five thousand pounds.'

'Christ.' It was the only way. 'That's a fair chunk of bread.'

'You'll help?'

I shrugged. 'No choice.'

'Is there anything else you should know?'

'What's it look like, this . . . chess-set?'

Hamilton sighed. 'It was the only work of its kind produced by the House of Fabergé. The pieces are carved in black opal and topaz. Each queen is set with a rose diamond for a crown. Every other piece carries a cabochon ruby.'

'I'm getting to believe you.' I stood up. 'Must've had a few bob, your wife's lot.'

For a moment Hamilton looked narked. 'The base of each piece is engraved with the initials HW.'

'Right.' I took my gear out of the plastic bag. 'D'you mind?'

Hamilton took a card from his wallet. 'My address. Call me at any time.'

I scribbled a number for him. 'Mine.'

He led me to the door, head bowed, hands behind his back like the Duke only smaller.

'If you find the film, would you be good enough to . . . please deliver it to me. Personally. It's important that I see it first.'

He'd spoken low. Not low enough for the others to have missed it.

Ten

Back in the gaff I chucked off my clothes and dropped face-down on the bed, but within minutes the drizzle in my stomach had me on my knees at the bog like some white-faced Moslem. Afterwards I cleaned myself up and dressed in shirt and slacks, casual, free as a football kicked out of touch.

Out there was a man with fair hair. His name was Cain and he was thinking of me.

The rest rolled in my skull like gas. Some pratt had nicked a chess-set and sitting on top was a film. Down in Whitehall a Jock and two Tories were that keen to get it back they'd called off the dogs so I could nick it. Not the chess-set. The film. Now those chess-men were worth a few bob, maybe as much as ten grand on the quiet side of the market, and they might just fall into the wrong hands if I boxed clever. It had been a week since the snatch and the goods couldn't've got that far, because unless trade had changed in nine months there weren't many dealers with asbestos for skin.

And Quist.

What did he owe Cain? Because never mind what Quist said, Cain didn't make friends. So maybe the only chance of a laugh was Quist collecting the carver too, and even that would've been funnier if I hadn't been top of the list myself. But either way, Cain wouldn't hit for ten days. I needed one thousand pounds a day.

It was turned seven when I stepped out, picking a path through the motors down Goodge Street to the Northern Line. A fair head in the lift set the fuses popping in my chest till I shut my eyes and thought of Greenland, which although it may not call stop as fast as a dive under a train, can slow the pulse to a ton and a half. I was calm when I got out at Camden Town, weaving fast through the micks outside the fish-and-chip shop and up Camden Road towards Kalinikou's place. The arches were dark and wet, and the yard looked like the Co-op after the summer sale. The word must've spread because the gannets had already nicked everything they could shift with two hands. The gates leaned drunk where they'd smashed the lock, and come tomorrow the heavies would roll up in their vans to collect what they'd left today. The 1300 stood where I'd left it the day before, complete with tyres and mirrors, not that I cared. They could pinch the whole motor in ten days if I was unlucky, on account of I wouldn't need it where Mister Cain reckoned to send me. I had bother getting it started, then rolled up Kentish Town Road and turned left at Gordon House Road for the Royal Free.

Lacey was awake, his eye still glowing. I could hardly credit it but he seemed to have improved. I mean, his mind was steadier and his hate had condensed into a lump that radiated like nuclear waste.

I sat down. 'Shiv?'

'What d'you want?'

'Christ.' I shrugged. 'Just come to see you.'

'Yeah.'

'Anything I can get you?'

'No.'

'Nothing at all? Sure?'

'Sure.' He sneered. 'The Law's looking after me.'

I did a quick take over my shoulder. 'They still here?'

'Gone. Now.'

I breathed. 'What'd they want?'

'What do they ever want?' He spoke into the pillow.

'They got no call on you.' I blinked. 'Have they?'

'No?' He turned his eye. 'How about murder?'

'What?'

'Cora.'

'Sorry.' I looked at my feet. 'Sorry.'

'Me too.'

'How'd . . . it happen?'

The skin round his eye tangled. 'Petrol bomb. A fucking Molotov through the window.'

'Sorry.'

He moved his head from side to side. 'Don't be sorry. Not for me. Not for her.' He gasped for air. 'You save your sympathy for them. By Christ they'll need it.'

I leaned close. 'Shiv. Forget it. Don't act stupid.'

If he'd been fit he'd've laid one on me. 'You know nothing. Nothing.' His chest jerked. 'I'll set the record straight.'

I needed more. 'Why'd they do it?'

He started to laugh but it cracked into a cough that ploughed lines in his cheeks. 'The bracelet.'

'Who?'

'Never bloody mind who. Just mark my words.'

'That South London firm, was it?'

'I'll tell you something.' A hand spidered out of the bed and snatched my wrist. 'I will personally . . . strangle that bastard . . .'

'Who, Shiv?'

'And every one of his soldiers.'

I unhooked my wrist. 'Lie back, eh? In your state you won't be doing anything to anybody.'

His face mashed with pain. 'I'll be out sooner than you think for.'

'I hope so.' And it looked like he wouldn't be taking anybody else with him.

A nurse looked round the screen. 'Please. Mr Lacey needs rest.'

'OK. Mind how you go, Shiv.'

I was glad I hadn't done it.

I couldn't get within a quarter-mile of Soho Square it was

that jammed. It being a Friday it seemed the swedes had flown in to poke sticks at the locals who of course were taking it as per normal, except for them that relied on tourists for picking, and there was more than a brace of them lurking in doorways. Dean Street was solid and I wound up walking in the road close to the motors to avoid getting trampled. A pair of blokes fell out of Scotch's as I arrived and I didn't like the taste of that on account of they smelled foreign and I remembered a time when Georgie Farmer might've got out of Parkhurst easier than a swede might've got into Scotch's. Downstairs it was all go, a knot of shapes blocking the light from the bar, the giggle of birds and the tinkle of bottles. I collared the barman.

'Where's Scotch?' He was telling me Scotch had left the country when the office door opened. 'Save it.' It was four steps to the office. Scotch stood in his best suit, one hand on the doorknob. 'I wanna talk to you.'

His wrinkles splintered. 'Come in.' He shut the door behind me.

'Proud of yourself, are you?'

'Harry . . .'

'Don't Harry me, you beat-up bag of offal. You knew all the time.'

He limped to the booze cabinet. 'Droppa mother's?'

'Put a glass near me and I'll piss in it.'

He poured a drink. 'OK. I know about this bloke Cain. The word's been around more'n a month.' He turned. 'What could I do? You're poison, Harry.' He swallowed a mouthful of gin. 'I don't want you seen in my place.'

'Don't fret, sweetie-pie.' I sneered. 'I shan't show a light longer than I've got to. But if you wanna lose me you're going to have to make a few answers or I'll stick up a sign saying Harry Grant Sleeps Here.'

He splashed another four fingers into his glass. 'Ask. Then go.'

That stung.

'Fine.' I kept one hand on the doorknob. 'Remember a bloke called Lacey? Shiv Lacey?'

Scotch twitched. 'What about him?'

'He's idling in the Royal Free with a face like roast pork and no wife. Who did it?'

He was quick to look away. 'How should I know?'

'You know on account of you've hung about this manor watching life's parade these past nine months while I've been attending to other business. Who did it?'

Scotch rubbed his eyes. 'Harry. It's all different since you went. Bad times, like I said.' He lowered his backside to the edge of the desk. 'All the old firms've changed. They change faster than snap these days.'

'You take all the time you like.' I pointed at his face. 'I tell you I won't let you be till you tell me what I want to know.' I leaned against the door, arms folded. 'Lemme help. Lacey flogged me the prettiest set of sparklers you ever saw. He was in a hurry. Then somebody chucked a cocktail into his kip. From what he says I do not need the brain of an Einstein to compute the connection between these two events. So where'd he nick the sparklers?'

'Who knows?'

'Scotch,' I sighed, 'I had you down for a regular mucker, you know? Good old Scotch. Pity. I know a certain party that will indubitably draw his own conclusions about the time I spend round here, especially when I go on and on about good old Scotch before I die.'

Scotch slammed his glass on the desk. 'I oughta take you apart.'

'You ought to,' I agreed. 'I'm a mean sod. No heart. When I go all my ex-mates go with me. How's that for straight-up cussedness? Course, if you don't fancy the white wings just yet you can always give me a lead.'

Scotch slumped. 'I can only say what I know.'

'That, mate, is a daft remark. Even for you.'

I waited. 'Lacey . . .' he puffed his cheeks, 'got mixed up with this firm South of the river. Run by a party name of Beau.'

'Beau?'

'Short for Beauregard. It's French.'

'Go on.' I felt for a cigar.

'Well, this Beau . . . nobody seen him coming. Suddenly he was there, about six months ago this was. As time goes by the firm gets bigger. First it's Fulham, then the Bush, then the Harrow Road, and suddenly, four months ago, his soldiers start showing the knuckle up West . . .'

'And?'

Scotch sat down. 'You know as well as me he couldn't've done it five years ago, what with Reggie and the Colonel tending the manor. But these days it's easy, not much opposition. He's into everything, drugs, bookies, cat-houses, you name it, he's got twenty. The firm's a bloody octopus. You never know who you're talking to, every second layabout's on the payroll.'

I was starting to suss the layout. 'Protection?'

'He's murdered private enterprise . . .'

'Protection?'

He looked at me. 'He's been in here. He knows a going concern when he sees it.'

'You wouldn't.' I watched his face.

'Fucking right I wouldn't.' Scotch looked grim. 'I gotta be ready for him when he comes, though.'

'You better be readier than Lacey, sweetheart.'

He squinted at me. 'Haven't you got bother enough? It's not your problem. Looking for a hero's funeral, are you?'

I shrugged. 'Maybe they'll bury me in Westminster Abbey.'

'Leave off, Harry.' He stood up. 'Get out while you can.'

I tapped his chest. 'Say more about this Beauregard. What's he like? As a bloke, I mean?'

'Fancies himself. Spends time getting photographed at Claridges with dukes and that. They don't know the half of it.'

I was puzzled. 'Would he bother to bust a peter?'

'Depends. Not for the money, he's got better sources. Only for something special, something he wanted.'

'Got a peter-man on the books, has he?'

Scotch sipped. 'I told you. He's got twenty of everything,

and that goes for peter-men. If you say Lacey flogged you sparklers he must've nicked them off of Beau.' He shook his head. 'Stupid bugger, Lacey. Dresses like John Wayne, acts like Mickey Mouse. He had it coming.'

'Go and take a look at him if that's what you think.'

'Seen it all before.' He set his glass down. 'You think that's new? The stories I could tell you.'

'How do I get to this Beau?'

'You better go.'

'Where do I find him?'

Scotch was moving towards the door. 'Remember Maisie Dixon? Ask her. She knows. You'll find her in the Coachman every night. Just don't hang about here.'

I opened the door. 'You will be double chuffed to hear that I do not intend to disport my handsome person about this manor no more.' I thought. 'And if you happen to sight my old mate Crab tell him he better stop awake, on account of one day I shall be wanting a little chat with him.'

Scotch was staring into his glass when I left.

I didn't recognize Maisie at first. She was sitting in the corner of the Coachman, stretched taut as a drumskin, juggling a glass from one hand to the other. Her cheeks were scarlet and her eyes were sort of wild, skittering in circles from the door to the bar and back again. I got two glasses of G&T and sat down next to her.

'Hullo, Maisie.'

She jumped like I'd dropped ice down her back. Something like recognition flickered in her face. 'Buy me a drink.'

'I just did.'

Gin slopped on the table as she raised the glass, and she drank deep and full with her eyes shut.

'Get me another.'

While I stood at the bar I watched her looking at the door again. 'Expecting somebody?'

'Somebody.'

'Anyone I know?' She didn't answer. 'Maisie. Scotch says you can tell me where to find this Beauregard, the one from

South of the river.'

She stared at me for ten seconds. 'Did he?'

'Can you?'

She looked at the door. 'For Christsake get me another drink.'

There was a feller sitting with her when I took the drinks back. A dapper little bloke who smiled a lot. Maisie was eating his face with her eyes.

'Got it?'

He grinned. 'You oughta learn to relax.'

'Please.' She caught his sleeve. 'Have you got it?' She mauled the inside of her handbag. 'Here.' She waved a roll of notes. 'Give it to me.'

I nodded at the little feller. 'Who's he?'

They ignored me. He took the money with one hand and passed something to Maisie with the other. She stood up, so I held her arm.

'Maisie. Where can I find this Beauregard?'

'How would I know?' She tried to move but I tightened my grip.

'Tell.'

She turned to face me, suddenly calm. 'You know what he did to me? Do you?' She rolled up her sleeve and flexed her hand so the needle-marks on her arm swelled. 'Then he dropped me. For one of his tarts from Belgravia. Some blue-blooded snot-nosed little bitch slumming as a stripper at the Alhambra.' She snapped her arm back. 'Give him my love.'

The little bloke yawned.

'Takes all types. Fancy a drink?'

I looked at him. 'Why not? Large mother's.'

I was smiling when he got back. 'All types,' he told me again. 'Nice bird, Maisie. A bit . . . nervous,' he grinned, 'know what I mean?'

'Well, I guess it gets them like that after a bit, doesn't it?' I stood up, glass in hand. 'Cheers.' I emptied my gin over his head and left.

I was thinking about Beauregard on the way to Charlotte Street. Ten grand can't be that difficult to come by. All you need is fifty thousand unoccupied phone booths and a lot of very dark nights.

Eleven

Around midnight you'd never believe Streatham High Road was the same place you'd bought your breakfast kippers. I'd guess the Vegas Strip is longer, and a nod there might cost you a hundred grand, but the feeling's the same. Technicolor dream-signs wash the night, strokes of electric sunlight howling Bingo, Wimpeys, Casino, Fun-Palace and Odeon. I didn't get too near the Alhambra. The Spanish castle flung light like a tidal-wave, bleaching the blacktop as far as the reservation, and a feller like a grizzly in a braided cap was sunning himself on the pavement. I stopped in the motor, head down, parked across the street with the light lapping the retreads. The action looked good. Punters strolled in like Gene Kelly and out like Boris Karloff so there were no prizes for guessing who was on top. One Saturday-night maverick was carried out by Percy and the grizzly, nothing nasty, it was just that his feet were pointing away from the direction he wanted. The other two scrummed close and whispered words in his shell-like till he shuffled off South. There's more than one way of bouncing the boy that breaks the bank.

Nine days.

About twelve this motor glided to the kerb. It must've been thirty feet long, a Cadillac white as winter and glossed like ice till the difference between steel and glass wasn't worth trying to see. While I watched this miracle of the motor-trade the driver got out to stretch his legs. He was short, showing shovels for shoulders and a waist nipped by a double-breasted jacket. He circled the bonnet and leaned on the passenger's window, nattering to the man inside. The door opened and another feller unwrapped himself, resting an elbow on the car roof like it was bar-height in a boozer. He might've been big but he'd been last in the queue when the angels gave out necks and foreheads, the top of his head showing even bristle all the way to his eyebrows. Still, maybe this Bullet-head had a sweet nature. They knew each other well, these two. They didn't bother smiling while they talked, their jokes were short, their laughs shorter, and I wasn't betting on their tempers. Interesting, but nothing to do with me. Till I saw Felix.

Elegant, one hand holding her hem off the pavement, she emerged with a lean-looking character whose shirt glistened against his tan. You could tell he was fit by the way he stood. The pair leaning on the Caddie dropped their fag-butts and made hullo signals. Felix swopped a word with the short guy while the boyfriend laughed at a joke from Bullet-head and dropped a friendly punch on his chest. Short-arse opened the door and got them settled, then walked round and climbed in the front. The Cadillac started with a thunderclap that carried over the noise of the traffic. I kicked the 1300 to life and raced down the East carriageway to the lights, doing a Fangio in the face of the river of Minis rolling North. You couldn't lose the Caddie. I stayed two cars behind and let them lead North, crossing the river at Vauxhall Bridge, straight up and through the mess at Victoria on to Grosvenor Place. At Hyde Park Corner the Cadillac nosed round the island and down Piccadilly; I nearly lost them when they turned down a side-street. From then on I lingered on account of there wasn't much in the way of lights or passing cars to hold their eyes. We passed the Curzon, pushing deeper into Mayfair round the old-fashioned buildings with bow-fronts. They stopped in Waverton Street.

There was a choice. I could wait behind while they parked, allowing Felix to recognize the classical lines of my body while the others reduced it to ruins, or I could squeeze past with head low in the hope she'd keep her nose pointing the same way as her knees. The off-side wheels of the 1300 bounced on the kerb as I passed but nobody spared a squint. A hundred yards up the road I found a mews, waited fifteen minutes, then locked up and strolled back.

The club was called Caligula's. Glass doors led to a foyer hung with snapshots of celebrities posing with the same guy in the same tuxedo, which I reckoned he'd bought about the time he was snapped with Tyrone Power. Some of the pictures were autographed. Climbing the stairs the music swelled till I stood in a noisy lobby where a bird posed by a counter taking coats and shaking her goodies for fivers. I dropped my raincoat and turned into the gents where I pumped a palmful of liquid soap from a dispenser, had a wash and combed my hair. Then I settled into my suit like a customer just nipped out for a pee, left the carsie shouting see you later, and shouldered the doors that lead to the action. The music closed round my head and the spin-ball over the dance floor shot darts into my eyes that set me fumbling for the wall. There weren't any lights except candles on the tables and a yellow drench on the padding of the bar-front opposite. A hand touched my arm and I looked into the snooty marbles of the head-waiter who was mouthing questions. I laughed, patted his arm and strolled towards a group at the bar.

I leaned on the padding and lifted someone's glass, grinning when the group laughed which was so often it hurt my face. My eyes were adjusting to the light, sorting out the shapes on the floor, when the barman ducked under the counter. I swallowed the dregs in the glass and asked for the same again. He nodded, delivered a cocktail to a chick with bare shoulders, then moved to the optics. He turned, forehead creased.

'What was it, sir?'

I looked impatient. 'Gin and tonic.' It hadn't been, but I flipped a quid and stopped expecting change after ten minutes.

The group made effective cover, swaying and noisy the way people act after a few. I cradled my gin and watched the tables. I spotted the short guy first because his face was in direct light from the candle. Bullet-head opposite caught the glow on his shirt-front while his bristle butted into the darkness. Felix sat at the next table, drumming her fingers, face turned towards the dance-floor while the boyfriend called for a menu. I didn't know how they normally acted but tonight they weren't on speaking terms. The music lifted like a rock off my shoulders and the mob on the floor broke into couples that drifted towards the tables. The boyfriend seemed restless, speaking over his shoulder to the short bloke while Felix smoked and studied her nail polish. The little man listened, nodded, and cut round the floor to the bar. I carried my drink to a low table and sat with my back to the diners. The small guy passed within three feet, swaggering fit to massacre the first toddler to cross his path. He really was short, less than five feet, too tall to make a career of it and too small to escape comment. I thought he might find bother getting served but the barman saw him coming, cleared a space forward of the counter and tried not to stoop to hear the order. Short-arse was all too aware of his height, I mean he was acting ten feet tall, feet apart, shoulders flexing, hands on hips like Crusoe standing over Friday. The barman gave him two cigars and Short-arse marched back and handed them to his guv'nor. Then he climbed back on his chair and sat with arms folded watching the birds. He was the sort of gnome who'd pinch the arse of the biggest redhead and ask her to dance. And he was the sort of gnome the biggest redhead would dance with. Still, being little he probably had a thing about women with a lot to offer.

The head-waiter was galloping a flunkey towards the boyfriend's table, hand under his elbow, rabbitting nastily in his earhole so you could almost hear him saying if you don't look after this mob I'll have you washing dishes before you can say Colonel Kray. They surrounded the table, bowing and sweating and emptying ashtrays while the head-waiter introduced the other bloke. The boyfriend asked a question. The waiter bent over the menu, nodding and smiling and trying to staunch the sweat in his eyes. It was a long discussion. The boyfriend gestured a lot while the waiter grinned and scribbled and scribbled and grinned, which was very sensible. Felix ignored the whole display. The head-waiter dragged a second scivvy to Bullet-head's table. Short-arse didn't even raise his eyes to order, and anyway the waiter was more bothered about Bullet-head, who, sitting down, was taller than the waiter standing up. Eventually the staff left like a herd of deer scared off a water-hole.

The music crashed again as I eased out of my chair to get another drink. Most of the drinkers had scattered to the tables so I sat down the dark end of the bar tracing lines in the wet on my glass. A man and a girl stopped by Felix's table for a natter. The boyfriend didn't get up and didn't introduce Felix, who sat chin in hand watching the dancing while he addressed his eyes to the other bird who was wearing tasselled silk and not much else by the look of them. Her bloke was chuffed that any chick of his should excite attention from the boyfriend and seemed to be nudging her closer so this man among men might not miss anything he would later regret. He needn't have worried because this Champ of Charver was not the regretting type. He was on his feet and guiding the bird to the dance-floor before her partner could wish her luck. Like I said, the boyfriend was a very healthy specimen of what used to be called Manhood before the seven-stone weaklings started chucking the sand back. He was lithe and confident, drawing glances from birds already spoken for. Silk Tassel's partner looked uncertain as he pulled up a chair to speak to Felix. She mouthed one word that stopped him mid-squat. He straightened, tried to smile, and edged back to his own table. Felix stubbed her fag, gathered her shawl and left. The boyfriend didn't see her go.

'Menu, sir?' The head-waiter dropped an encyclopedia on the bar-top, acting like he ought to attend to more important visitors. 'Might I recommend the Lobster Thermidor?'

'You might.' I opened the menu and gazed upon words printed over scenes of Romans having orgies.

'When you're ready, sir.' He glided away.

The music changed and the boyfriend walked Silk Tassel to his table. He didn't look amazed it was empty. He got the bird settled and dragged a chair round to sit thigh to thigh.

The head-waiter was watching me. I did not intend to nosh a lobster and give the boyfriend's soldiers time to pick their teeth before they picked mine. It was time for action. I beckoned the barman.

'That mob over there.' He followed my nod. 'Who are they?' He polished a glass. 'Customers, sir.'

'Sure.' I didn't want to excite him. 'Regulars, are they?'

'You could say that.' He moved away.

'Just a minute. What's his name, the bloke with the tan?'

'His name?'

'His name.'

He swallowed. 'That . . . that's, er . . . Mr Cohen, I believe. If you'll . . .'

'First name?'

He'd left one hand on the bar like I'd nailed it down. 'Um, I think . . . well, I've heard them call him, er, Beau.'

When I looked round the barman was having a whisper with the head-waiter and the sizzle down my spine said it was quitting time for H. Grant, who is of course smart enough to walk out slow and cause no ripples. I got my coat from the bird in the lobby, thankful to escape the music, and ducked into the carsie on the way out. It reminded me of hospitals, white tiles and the hum of airconditioning. The urinal was at the end of the room, hidden behind the last of the cubicles. While I stood there I heard the door open and thought no more till I stepped down to leave.

Short-arse was resting an elbow on a basin, one leg crossed over the other. Bullet-head folded his arms, smiling like a hammerhead shark. 'Ja-ja.'

I zipped up. 'Pip-pip.'

Short-arse moved into the space between the basins and the cubicles, hands behind his back.

'Luigi says you was expressing more than a mild and passing interest in the welfare of certain of his guests tonight.'

'Eh?'

Bullet-head straightened, growing like a baobab. 'Qvestions.

You ask too many qvestions.'

I pointed at him. 'You are Martin Bormann and I claim the prize. Now, if I don't scarper I shall miss "This Is Your Life".'

'Mr Cohen would be grateful if you saw fit to join him for a little bit of a rabbit.' Short-arse moved forward.

'What is this?' I backed against the tiles. '"Candid Camera"?'

'Pliss,' said Bullet-head. He'd got a scar on his forehead and hadn't been handsome before either. 'To come with me and Charlie. Mr Cohen does not like the waiting games.'

I turned a tap. 'Your sauerkraut will be getting cold.'

Charlie looked up at Bullet-head. 'He's worried about our dinners. Nice feller. Isn't he, Hermann? Speaking personally, I'd say it was a pleasure to make the acquaintance of a man so concerned with everyone's welfare.'

'It's a welfare state,' I told him.

'But the trouble with that sort is they forget to look after themselves. I mean, you can tell by looking at him, can't you?'

'Is terrible thin.'

'That's right, Hermann. Hasn't had a good dinner in years, I'd say.' He rolled on his heels. 'Very out of condition, I should think.'

'I'm still growing,' I said. 'Unlike some people I could mention. What do they call you? The Poisoned Dwarf?'

Charlie's knife sparked as the door bounced open.

'Not yet.'

Cohen held a cigar in his right hand. The vertical lines forming in his tan said he was past forty.

'Sorry, Mr Cohen.' Charlie dropped the knife in his pocket. 'We was just bringing him in.'

I said, 'King Cohen, I presume?'

Cohen separated his soldiers. He wore a ring on every finger and heavy gold links on his cuffs. 'Luigi says you're some kind of nark.'

'Me?' The chuckle died in my chest. 'I wouldn't chew Old Bill's ear if you served it with salad.'

'Thought I'd check first.' I could see he'd made up his mind. He held out a hand. 'Car keys.' Charlie gave him a bunch on a ring. 'Be at my place by ten, I want to talk to you.' He patted the wall-tiles. 'And don't leave litter. Luigi doesn't like it.'

'Oy,' I called. 'Why not drop Laurel and Hardy at Bertram Mills on the way?'

The door slammed.

Hermann was grinning. I turned back to the basin while he fitted a bronze knuckle-duster over a fist like a boulder.

'Let me get this straight.' I pumped the soap dispenser, 'First Charlie bites them on the shin, right? Then what do you do? Peel their tattoos for lampshades?'

Hermann's bellow shook the doors. The bronze on his fist shone as he lifted it high over his head. I flipped sideways and let him have a handful of liquid soap in the eyes just as the duster hit the basin. The porcelain split down the middle like glass, leaving a shaft on each wall-bracket. I got my shoulder into the small of Hermann's back as he clawed at his eyes, using the weight of his swing to throw him into a whirl. He crashed backwards into the cubicle door, splintering the woodwork and taking the ironmongery with him. It was a mess, the wood, Hermann and the bog indistinguishable one from the other. Charlie crouched. I shot my cuffs, feeling the remains of the basin jab me in the back.

'Which one are you?' I panted. 'Grumpy?'

Charlie twisted his lips and charged like a chimp gone berserk, knife outstretched. I skipped left, leaving a foot in his path. He'd forgotten about the shafts of porcelain on the wall.

I collided with an elderly party just outside the door. He was pissed and his specs were crooked.

'Shouldn't go in there,' I told him. 'Bloody mess. Some people just can't hold their booze.'

It took thirty seconds to find the 1300 and get out of the mews.

Twelve

'Mr Grant?'

It was Sunday night and I was calculating how much leather I'd left on the pavement that day.

'Yeah.'

'I wondered . . .' said Hamilton, 'if you'd mind coming to my house for an hour?'

'What for?'

'I would, er, prefer to explain when you arrive. Can you come now? Is it awfully inconvenient?'

I'd been lying on the bed balancing a glass of mother's on my chest. The sound of the phone had made me flinch and a drop of gin had splashed on my shirt. I had a wash and climbed into my new suit; no point dressing like a villain, I mean, Hamilton might fire me in which case I would need my best gear to convince the Holy Ghost I deserved welcome.

Eight days.

Cadogan Place isn't just posh. When you stop in Sloane Street and look across the grass you realize you're in the presence of Authority and I don't mean the fuzz or anything crude as that. This is the Authority of History, you might say, of generations who could gain as much by lifting a finger as the Law could by jumping on your back and beating you to death. Cadogan Place can kill with a twitch of an upturned nostril. On the North you've got Carlton Tower. You can't even talk to the doorman there. He stands in his flash brown outfit looking like the Duke of Marlborough directing the Battle of Agincourt. He sniffs, and taxis grapple down Knightsbridge for the privilege of wiping his nose. On the West side of Sloane Street are shops with dark windows showing maybe just a symbol etched in gold, the theory being if you're there at all you know you can afford it so there's no point putting it on display. These shops and the Carlton Tower face a park which is fenced off so the herberts don't get to dirty the grass with their leathers. Course, the value of grass being what it is these days they've had to build a car-park under the green but the entrance is so clever you could live there for years without spotting it. Then, on the East side facing the lawns, is this row of houses, six storeys of the kind of influence that doesn't need tiaras to get results. Hamilton lived about the middle of the terrace.

I stood on the porch adjusting my jacket. The bell wasn't what you'd expect, no clever tunes, just the sound of a single chime deep inside the house. I was anticipating a flunkey like the doorman at the Carlton Tower and was therefore double struck to see Hamilton stood on the mat like any ordinary berk come to swat the Jehovah's Witnesses. His manner was eager and he shook my hand.

'Mr Grant. Good of you to spare the time.'

He led me into a hall like a Paramount set. A massively curled staircase swept skywards on the left, and the doors on both sides were eight feet tall, boxed inside pilasters.

'Handsome drop of semi, Mr H.'

He looked pleased. 'Do you like it?'

As if that was a cue a woman appeared on the half-landing. She wore a plain skirt and sweater with a single string of pearls, but it was the bird with her that wowed me. She was adjusting a leather hat over blonde hair, descending the steps like she needed an escort of Fred Astaires. And that wasn't all. She sported a pair of chestnut leather trousers cut high enough to dazzle the audience with the sweep of waist and hip, divided down the front by a family-sized steel zip with a ring-fastener hung with medallions. Her shirt was a vicar's nightmare, one shoulder draped with a jacket to match her trousers.

Felix.

The women stopped in the hall, Felix's medallions tinkling as she rested her weight on one hip. Hamilton stretched an arm.

'Er, Marion, my wife. This is Mr Grant.' Tinkle. 'And Felicity Bellingham.' They smiled. 'Mr Grant has agreed to . . . help us get the Fabergé back.'

Mrs Hamilton inspected me. 'I hope Roger has explained how important the Fabergé is to us, Mr Grant. It's been in my family for many years. It was commissioned by Leopold de Rothschild as a gift for my grandfather.'

'Oh.'

She opened the door for Felix, one hand at her elbow.

'Do give my love to your mother, won't you? I wish she'd move back to Town. Life's been so dull since they left. Are you seeing them soon?'

'Probably.' Felix kissed Hamilton's cheek. 'See you soon, Roger. Marion.' The women embraced.

'Come to dinner sometime,' said Hamilton. 'Bring a boyfriend.'

Felix inclined her head. 'I'd like that.'

Mrs Hamilton shut the door. 'I'll leave you to it.' She climbed the stairs. 'Shout if you want anything.'

'Shall we go in?' Hamilton stepped back.

The lounge was what you'd expect, bay windows draped in royal blue, walls hung with paintings. There was one canvas about ten feet long on the end wall showing a group of gays having their tea round a low table.

'Hockney,' said Hamilton. 'Do you like it?'

'Yes.'

McLeod was standing with one hand on the back of a couch that looked like it could swallow us all.

'G'd evening.' He looked out of place in his grubby roll-neck.

'Hullo.'

'Drink?' Hamilton poised at a sideboard under the long painting.

'Cheers. G & T'll suit me fine.'

I lowered myself into the couch while Hamilton poured the drinks. He perched on the arm of an easy chair, considered the glass in his hand and reached for his Rennies.

'I've, er, discussed the subject with my colleagues, and we've . . . decided that, well, the importance of your role wasn't . . . emphasized enough on Friday.' He swung his foot, tracing furrows in the carpet.

'Oh?'

McLeod twisted on the couch, one foot tucked against his thigh.

'There are some facts we've agreed ye should hear.'

'Where's this peter, then?'

'What?' McLeod frowned.

'The safe.'

They looked at each other.

'In the study.'

I followed Hamilton to a door on the far side of the hall. The study was small, maybe ten feet square, the window hung with the blue I'd seen in the lounge, a backdrop to a mahogany desk too big for the room. The peter stood against the inner wall, about four feet high, showing steel like the Graf Spee.

'It was picked,' said Hamilton. 'The CID tell me it's so outdated it would have been easy for the right man.'

'I've seen tougher nuts than that open like Sesame. There must be an army of peter-men fit enough to bust this and still get home for a good night's kip.' I thought of Felix. 'Where did you say you'd gone?'

'The Guildhall.' He opened he door. 'If you're satisfied, Mr Grant . . .'

Felix must've known Mrs H would be wearing most of her clobber to the Guildhall.

Back in the lounge Hamilton sipped his port and winced.

'Things have been going, um, wrong for the Bureau for some time, Mr Grant. You may remember Angola? The war could've been avoided in favour of – at worst – partition, had our advice been implemented.' He looked to McLeod for confirmation. 'Instead, our friends found their every move pre-empted by the other side.'

McLeod swilled his glass. 'That was spectacular, but on a smaller scale we lose ground by the day.'

'Then,' Hamilton looked uneasy, 'two months ago the people at the, er, FO heard a murmur from the East. There'd been one or two, um, overtures from an officer in the KGB who, er, wished to make his . . . resources available to the West.'

McLeod walked to the sideboard and poured himself a drink. 'He agreed to collaborate for three months before coming in.' The couch heaved like a sea-swell when he sat beside me.

'Three weeks ago,' said Hamilton, 'this . . . man was able to confirm our suspicions. He, er, produced proof of a leak from the . . . home side.' He stared into his glass. 'From the Bureau.'

McLeod ran a hand through his mane. 'He was arrested fifteen days ago. Before the FO was able to . . . help.'

There was a grandfather clock somewhere. I could hear the tock-plop from the couch. Hamilton and McLeod had as much soul as that clock, and I had eight days left.

'The source of the leak,' said Hamilton, 'was identified in some documents photographed by this . . . officer before his arrest. The film delivered here on the night of the burglary. Special Branch don't expect immediate identification through the film, but, well . . .'

I couldn't help feeling sorry for him whoever he was. Funny. They were going on about a feller already responsible for at least one man winding up on the slab in the Kultur Room but I felt more in common with him than these two. Maybe it was the axe poised over both of us.

Hamilton was speaking again.

'I know nothing about you, Mr Grant, except that, well,

judging by your relationship with the police . . .'

'I'm a villain?'

McLeod studied the marks on my face. 'I see ye're not a vicar, anyway.'

Hamilton gazed at his shoes. 'What I wanted to say was, um, while you may be accustomed to . . . casual violence – forgive me – the man we're after is probably more dangerous than anyone you've had to face so far.' He didn't know the half of it. 'You see, I have to warn you that this, er, person will certainly try to prevent you finding the film . . .' the door chime interrupted. Hamilton excused himself and went out backwards.

McLeod watched me. 'All right?'

'Fine.'

'I mean will ye cope?'

'Will you?' I folded my arms. 'I can take care of myself.'

Hamilton entered with Travis.

'Um, Michael's here.'

Travis looked rich and elegant, like the room. He stopped at the threshold, eyes moving from McLeod to me.

Hamilton backed to the sideboard. 'You must try some of this, Michael.' He raised a decanter knobbly as a hand-grenade. 'Just your thing, I think.'

'Thanks.' Travis sat down and arranged the creases in his trousers. He was still looking at McLeod and me.

'There.' Hamilton passed a glass. 'I, um, invited Mr Grant to give him the facts.'

'I see.' Travis shut his mouth in a tight line.

Hamilton sighed. 'Michael. I'm not prepared to involve an outsider in this situation without warning him.'

'It's best,' said McLeod.

Travis sipped. 'Yes.' He set his glass dead centre of the table at his elbow, eyes fixed on McLeod. 'What exactly have you told him?'

McLeod sat up. 'We told – '

'Roger?' Travis hadn't shifted his gaze.

Hamilton fiddled with his glass. 'Just that, um, well, why the film is so important . . .'

'Yes?'

'And that, er . . . to be careful.'

I listened to the clock while Travis studied each of us in turn.

McLeod cleared his throat.

'Have ye finished with Grant?'

Hamilton jumped. 'I think so.'

'I'll see him to the door, then.'

'Goodnight, Mr Grant.' Hamilton showed a hand. 'Thank you for being . . . patient. Remember what I've told you.'

'I'll call you.'

Travis watched McLeod lead me out.

McLeod left the lounge door open while we stood in the hall.

'Harry,' he whispered, 'sorry about the interruption, man.'

'OK.'

'Listen,' he caught my sleeve. 'Watch out for Travis. He's a dangerous child, understand? Rich and spiteful.' He raised his voice. 'Remember, when ye get the film it'll be quickest if ye pass it direct to me, all right?'

I stared back into the lounge. 'If you say.'

He shut the door behind me.

The window to the lounge was ajar and I heard them start shouting as I walked down the steps. I paused on the pavement but the voices weren't clear. Christ, what a fit-up. The film identified someone in the Bureau as a spy and it might've been one of them, judging by the hassle. Travis hadn't been invited because he didn't see things their way, but was that the only reason? If I was Travis I'd swear McLeod was putting words in Hamilton's mouth, but Hamilton was so deep you couldn't tell who was manipulating whom. Either way, they all hated each other and now I was the jam in the sandwich. Somebody was likely to wind up hanging by his ankles and you didn't have to be Mussolini to figure who. I crossed the street.

The flicker by the railings had me crouched and ready almost before I'd registered fair hair.

She laughed. 'Such style.'

'What d'you want?' I straightened.

She held her hat in one hand, a fist on each hip holding her jacket wide so you couldn't miss the quiver under her shirt.

'That was an ungallant remark, Mr Grant. It is Mr Grant, isn't it? I've been waiting a long time and I'm rather cold.' She took my arm. 'I thought you might buy me a drink.'

I took her hand off. 'Look, darlin. My name's not Grant, I'm tired and I wanna go home. And you'll be late for work.'

'I don't work on Sundays.'

'Go home then.'

She turned serious. 'If you're looking for the Fabergé I'm on your side, you know. I want to talk to you. Among other things.' She put her hand back. 'Perhaps you'd better take me home with you.'

'OK.' I sighed. 'Come and have a rabbit. Among other things.'

'Yes.'

We passed the Carlton Tower. 'You've got a very sexy face,' I told her.

'I know.'

'Mind you,' we stopped at the car, 'I fancied you better naked and covered in silver dust.'

'I can do better than that, Mr Grant. Shall we go?'

Thirteen

'It's not much but it's home.' I flicked the switch as she drifted through the door shrugging off the leather jacket.

'Charming.' Her voice fell flat. She dropped the jacket on the armchair and pivoted in the middle of the room, arms folded, one finger poised on the point of her chin. 'But lacking . . . flair?'

I tried to draw the curtains. 'How the other half lives, sweetheart.'

She dropped into the chair and swung her legs over the arm. 'Boasting? Or just complaining?' She wore oxblood boots with stacked heels.

'Telling.'

'Don't bother.'

'Drink?'

'All this and drinks too. Do I have a choice?'

'Light Ale,' I told her, 'or Light Ale.'

'Light Ale.'

I rinsed a pair of tumblers and poured her a foamer. She'd swallowed half a glass before I sat down.

'Cheers.'

'Am I supposed to be impressed, Willie?'

'What?'

'This.' She waved a hand at the room. 'You can't tell me a thing.'

'Course. I was forgetting. You've seen it all down at the

Alhambra. Real life.'

'You enjoyed that.'

'Like they say in the comics, what sends a dizzy deb like you to a slug-pit like that?'

'Love? No?' She held out her glass. 'Would you believe exhibitionism?'

I took her tumbler and refilled it in the kitchenette. 'It's OK, love. I'm already impressed. I mean if you wanna slow up on the Light I shan't hold it against you as they say.'

'Fuck off.'

'Is there no limit to this chick's solidarity with the criminal classes?' I poured another for myself and stood with my back to the window watching her trousers ripple with the swing of her boot. 'Debs like you are four a penny down the Commercial Road or didn't you know that?' I frowned. 'I mean, I don't suppose you're here because of me. Anyone would've done.'

Her boot would've found base if I hadn't turned in time. As it was she left a bruise the size of a cabbage on my thigh. I caught her ankle and heaved upwards. She slipped forward in the chair, pretty arse high over the arm, and I gripped both ankles in my left, bringing my right down hard on the leather stretched across her buttocks. It was a good sound. It made me realize how bad I'd wanted to do that and how bad I wanted to do it again. She was a knot of fury, hands grabbing, scratching, panting and cussing while the leather made short swishing sounds against the chair. She wrenched my head down, nails clawing for my face. I was straining out of reach when my nose touched hers. There was a lull, then she had my tongue, a deep bite slackening soft, fingers leaving my hair and sliding to my nape while I buried my mouth. We broke, and I watched the wide mouth, the lashes resting on her cheeks, the hair draped on the chair. My hand reached for hers. She drew back, lifted the hems of her trousers and unzipped her boots. They hit the mat, gaping. She eased from the chair and knelt at the head of the bed clutching a pillow to her middle.

'You were wrong.'

'Yeah.' I was slipping out of my gear.
'Only you would do.'
There were traces of silver in her pubic hair.

Well I may not be Errol Flynn but you'd got to be thick as a pile of blankets to ignore this chick's kink, and anyway her nails were painful. So I started acting higher and harder than the situation warranted and the trouble with that is you're like to get so you're doing it for real. A while later I lay back wondering how many more like this were hiding behind Belgravia drapes. She snuggled against me, head rising and falling with my chest.

'Hey.' She tapped my nose. 'Are you giving up?'

'Having a breather.' I wished I could get my cigars.

'Hmm.' She stretched. 'I was just turning on.'

I stroked her hair. 'Cow.'

She traced the scratches on my shoulders. 'Hurt?'

'Yes. Thank you.'

She bit my ear. 'Preview. You should see me on Mondays.'

'Can't wait.' I got up and found my cigars. 'Smoke?'

She shook her head. 'Why does the leading male always smoke afterwards?' She rolled on her back, knees raised. 'Replenishment?'

I watched the smoke-cloud. 'Nicotine.'

'Oh God.' She yawned. 'Why are men so prosaic?'

'Why don't women belt up?'

She giggled. 'Authority. I like that in a man.' She nibbled my ear again. 'D'you beat women, Willie?'

'Only when they nip my earholes and won't belt up.'

She nuzzled. 'The things I'm going to make you do. You'll see.'

'Yeah?'

'I'm serious, you bastard.' She watched me. 'You've no idea how awful it used to be. Gormless Guards. Pathetic. Christ how I longed to be out of it, away from my parents, away from people like the Hamiltons.'

'What's wrong with the Hamiltons?'

She snapped upright. 'What's wrong with them? I despise

them and everything they stand for.'

This was a well-worn road. 'Sounds a bit strong to me.'

She wasn't listening. 'Those people are all the same. Effete. Hard cash and soft hands. You can't know . . . how I longed to . . . to . . . break free.'

'And now you have. Every night at eleven-fifteen you strip for reps from Reading.'

She chuckled. 'That's a strong tone, Mr Grant. Do I detect a note of jealousy?' She slid over my hips. 'Don't get jealous, darling, I warn you. I'm a bitch when I know.' She wriggled her behind. 'Hmm. Who's waking up again? Who's turned on by jealousy?' She sat astride my knees and watched, hands stroking circles on my belly, stopping short each time.

Eight days.

'What is it?'

'Nothing.' I stared at the ceiling.

'Don't you want . . . ?'

'No.' I pressed her aside. 'You came to talk. So talk.' I started getting dressed.

'You bastard!' She whirled to the chair. 'How dare you?' She slapped her clothes to her chest. 'You back-street misfit. *You* dare turn *me* down?'

I zipped up. 'Talk.'

She stamped a foot into her boot. 'You – '

'Straight swop, darlin.' I was combing my hair. 'I want this chess-set. What do you want?'

'I want him dead.' She collapsed on the bed. 'No.' Her face was buried in the pillow. 'Not dead. Not dead.'

I sat next to her. 'Oy. Leave off. There isn't nobody worth those kind of tears.'

'Don't humour *me*!'

'I want this Fabergé. What do you want?'

'Very well, Lionheart.' She wiped her face. 'D'you know who's got it? Do you?'

'Beau Cohen.'

She blinked. 'A snooper too. Your talents spread really

wide, don't they? Perhaps one day you'll even be able to satisfy a woman.'

'I'm working on it. Now, I want the Fabergé and you want Big Beau planted. Common ground there at least.'

'I want him hurt.' She clenched her fists. 'I want to see him squirm.'

'Seems you want a few people hurt. You finished with the Hamiltons?'

She sneered. 'Stick to motives you understand.'

'So tell me how you want him skewered.'

She stood up, tucking in her shirt. 'He's wanted the Fabergé since I first told him about it. He'll keep it. Even if he can never show it, he will keep it.' She found her cigarettes. 'D'you follow that, little man? It represents . . . something unattainable.'

'Like you?'

'Shut your mouth.' She blew smoke at the ceiling. 'Take it from him. Take it.' Her shoulders hunched. 'Christ that will hurt him.'

'I'll need help.'

'You've got it.' She broke her fag in the ashtray. 'He thinks I'll crawl back. They always do.' She laughed but not with her face. 'Oh I'll crawl back. And behind his back I'll be laughing.' She faced me. 'Once you're near him I can lead you to the Fabergé. But you'll have to get close to him first. Can you do that?'

'I reckon.'

'How long?'

I nearly laughed. 'Long as it takes. No more'n eight days, I can tell you that.' I scratched my head. 'Listen. I got more snooping to do. D'you know if Beau sussed the market before he decided to keep the set?'

She frowned. 'Probably not. Why?'

'Well did he get the touch from a fence, then, anyone that might've heard about it?'

'No.' She thought. 'Wait. There was a boy called . . . Shiv, who used to hang around Beau. He got involved somehow. He came to me afterwards. He said he deserved a share. He was angry that Beau kept the Fabergé and he'd been to a fence, a sort of specialist dealing in rare pieces for collectors who can't get them legitimately. Anyway, Shiv wanted me to persuade Beau to sell it to this man. I laughed at him. Christ, if I had the chance again.'

'You got it.' I found my pen. 'D'you reckon this Shiv would've told the fence where the Fabergé was?'

'Not him. He hated anybody knowing he worked for somebody else.'

'This fence. Where do I find him?'

'Ealing, I think.' She frowned. 'His number reminded me of a date . . .'

'And Beau's?' She gave me two phone numbers. 'Fine. That's it for now.' She walked to the door. 'See you on Death Row.' I let her out. 'Come again, sweetheart. I can't promise I'll leave scars but if you ask politely I'll do my best.'

The flat of her hand stung.

I shrugged. 'Oh well. I got my memories, haven't I?'

I listened to her stamp down the stairs and bounce the front door hard against the wall. Then I sat down and poured myself four fingers of mother's.

It must've been five minutes before I remembered the crash of the door as she went out. She hadn't locked the front door. I hauled to my feet and took two steps down the stairs. There was something coming. I backed into the the gaff till my calves pressed against the chair. Not Cain, surely to Christ, not already? Again the sound, slight, a footstep, on the landing. The door swung inwards.

Quist.

Lips twisted, eyes pale. 'Harry, you're a bag of bloody nerves.'

I sat heavy on the arm of the chair. 'What d'you want?'

'Nothing.' His eyes flicked at the mess on the bed. 'Your bird left the door open. Thought I'd come and see how you were getting on.'

'Piss off.'

He drove his fists into his raincoat pockets. 'Having a right old wrestle, by the look of things.' He licked his lips. 'Nice drop of arse, that, I'll be bound. Good, was she, Harry?'

'You wouldn't recognize the difference.'

'Bit . . . irresponsible of you though. I mean, charvering away at a time like this.' He lit a fag and dropped the match on the mat. 'Still, I ask myself what I'd do in your place. Probably grab all the slap and tickle I could get in the time left to me.' He coughed. 'Let's see. How long is it now . . .'

'Quist.' I was still shaking when I walked to the door. 'Unless you got a warrant I suggest you scarper with all expedience. In fact, sod off and stop making bother for innocent citizens.'

He raised a hand, eyes narrowed behind his own smoke. 'I'm going. Not long though, is it? I should do something about it if I was you.'

I slammed the door behind him.

I drank near two-thirds of a bottle of Gilbey's before I climbed into the cold damp bed.

Fourteen

Time was closing like a pair of scissors and while my nerves fried my feet called stop, which as your psychologists will tell you, are the perfect ingredients for the Twitch Nervosa. I needed ten grand's worth of Fabergé and Beau Cohen kept the key next to his sun-lamp tan. I spent most of Monday swallowing fire from a bottle, plotting paths other than the one I knew I'd have to tread. It was a waste of time and by four in the afternoon I was back at the start-gate. Beau Cohen. As I squared up to the phone I reckoned I had one advantage. Cohen may not have been chuffed about Hermann and the Poisoned Dwarf but he couldn't help being impressed. I collected some coins and camped on the landing.

With English phones everyone's a first-time loser.

'Beau Cohen please.' It was my second try and the line clicked and whirred like snakes.

'Who are you?'

'Tell him it's the postman.'

'Even postmen got names, boy. Try spelling it if you're shy.'

'Tell him I met him Saturday night. I got a deal for him.'

'What kind of deal?'

'A fat bloody deal, and if he's not here inside ten seconds he's blown it, right?'

I heard him put the phone down.

'Yes?' Delivered like a bullet.

'I gotta parcel that will interest you, Cohen.'

'Who are you?'

I cleared my throat. 'Listen. I've been splashing a lotta sweat trying to reach you and pretty soon I'm going to recognize the hopelessness of it all.'

'Who are you?'

'You can call me Willie. You'll know me when you see me.'

'How's that?'

'I was in Caligula's Saturday night.'

'So was everybody.' He talked like he was waiting for a bus. 'Which one were you, the one in the tassels?'

'No. The one in the carsie.'

The phone crackled. 'You.'

'Me.'

'Listen.' I heard him draw on his cigar. 'I know a couple of people who'd like to see you again.'

I spoke fast and clipped. 'What, when they recover? No chance, feller. We're not boy scouts, Cohen. Your two amateurs are dead lucky they came out breathing. Next time we'll have them for wallpaper.'

'You better . . .'

'Save the sunshine.' I had him hooked. 'My people are looking to do a deal. D'you want in or not?'

'I'm yawning. You better shout already.'

'I gotta sample of something you'll wanna buy.'

'Hard or soft?'

'Jesus, you think I don't know my market? Soft, sweetheart, soft for Chrissake. Think I'd waste good Horse on a schmuck like you?' I waited. 'Look, this conversation's a drag. Why don't you just forget . . .'

'Hang about.' He said it too quick. He put his hand over the phone and shouted at someone. Then: 'I don't deal in ounces. How much've you got?'

I sighed. 'Who the fuck d'you think you are, you jumped-up schmutter-merchant? You questioning me? Christ Almighty, you scoop the Oscar for Comic of the Year, you know that?' I started to snap. 'Look, my people must've got it wrong. Just forget it, OK? I'll – '

'Hey you.'

'Willie. My name is Willie.'

'OK. I don't say I want in, but if you want to talk . . .'

'I told you, it's a drag. My jaw aches.'

'If you want to talk I'm at the A-One Sauna every Tuesday afternoon.'

'Yeah. Well, maybe I'll drop by if I'm round the manor. Maybe see you maybe won't.'

'Putney High Street. Three o'clock.'

I let him hear my fingers drum. 'Sure. But don't get too steamed, baby. If your rating's good we might make a deal but if I was you I wouldn't stake a mortgage on it.'

'My . . . what?'

'Your rating, pretzel. You're in the Big League now, feller. People are . . . careful. Know what I mean?'

'Listen – '

'And Cohen,' I whispered, 'leave your soldiers home, OK? Otherwise I swear we'll split you from here to Rejkyavik.'

I dropped into the cushions, reaching for the bottle. If I blew it tomorrow I'd save Cain the bother because he'd only have to wipe the blood off the tiles. It was getting difficult to light cigars. Not that I fancied smoking. Or eating. All I wanted was to pour comfort down my throat till it burned holes in my chest. So I sat there while the day gloomed and the gin sank and my thoughts turned so metaphysical I couldn't read the label with the light on.

The phone had me out of my seat and following my hair to the ceiling.

'What?'

'Mr Grant? Roger Hamilton.'

'Oh Christ.' I ran a hand over my eyes.

'Mr Grant?'

I started laughing. 'Hullo hullo.' I was holding my ribs. 'How's Cadogan Square? Making a living are we? Scraping a crust?'

'Mr Grant. Please.' My arms were numb. 'I'm in the office with Travis and McLeod. We must speak to you.'

'Let it lie, Hamilton. It's Monday. Monday the sixteenth. I never work on Monday the sixteenth, didn't they tell you that?'

He was trying to be patient.

'Something, er, something has come up. We must – please – discuss it.'

I giggled. 'Discuss away, Roger old chap. Old bean. Mister Belgravia. I'm for kip. Roger and out . . .'

'Grant. We must . . . agree tactics for the meeting tomorrow.'

'You do that, Roger old pal. You do that, on account of I'm busy tomorrow.'

'Exactly.'

I snatched at thoughts like flies. 'Eh?' Clicks and noises down the phone. 'Jesus! You bastard. You tapped my phone! You had my bloody phone tapped!'

'Shall we say, er, within half an hour? Will that suit you?'

Seven days. My breath stank. I tripped over the mat and lay there calling death on Hamilton, on Cohen, on Quist, and on Cain, Cain, Cain.

I don't remember getting to Whitehall but the street door was ajar and I cussed when I fell on the landing. Footsteps. Feet.

'C'mon, Harry.' McLeod hooked me off the floor. 'We're waiting on ye.'

He dragged me up the last flight and into the office.

Hamilton sat rigid behind the desk, face lit by the lamp at his elbow. Travis leaned on the mantlepiece, one hand in his pocket.

'Asshole.' I slumped in a chair.

Hamilton didn't blink. 'We must agree . . . strategy for tomorrow, gentlemen.'

McLeod pulled up a chair and shook a torn fag-packet at me. I fingered the paper till he took one out, lit it and placed it between my lips.

'Bastards.' The room took a second to catch a shake of the head.

'Who is Cohen?'

I tried to pin Travis with my eyes. 'Who invited . . . Leslie Howard?' I was amazed by my wit. 'Leslie Howard.'

'Ten minutes.' Travis spoke through his teeth. 'All I need is ten minutes alone with him.'

McLeod took the cigarette from his mouth, the creases in his face darkening.

Hamilton said: 'Michael.' Travis backed off reluctantly as Hamilton rested his elbows on the desk. 'Who is the man Cohen?'

'A lead, I dunno.'

'To the Fabergé?'

'Maybe.'

Travis moved close again. 'He's covering. Roger, he's covering.' He leaned over my chair. 'Has Cohen got the Fabergé?' I ignored him. 'Well?' I tried to peer round him but he blocked my view. 'You'll talk, Mister Grant. Eventually.'

I leaned sideways. 'Hamilton. Tell this . . . tell your bell-hop to save the Nazi bit for dossers and schoolboys, eh? They don't hit back.'

Travis's silhouette went rigid. 'Careful . . .' His voice was soft.

'You're in my way,' I told him.

'Michael.'

Travis spoke over his shoulder. 'McLeod. Get a bottle. He'll sing an aria for another drink.'

My fingers tightened on the arm of the chair.

'Harry.' McLeod spoke close to my ear. 'No.'

Travis sneered. 'Will you talk for me, Grant? Harry? I'll buy you a double if you do.'

'Michael.' Hamilton stood. Travis moved back to the wall without looking behind him. Hamilton coughed. 'Who is Cohen?'

I buried my face in my hands, trying to stop ahead. 'I told you. A lead. Maybe not.' My eyes burned my palms. 'He might know who's got the film.'

'How long will it take to find out?'

'How the hell do I know?' I wiped my face. 'Not by tomorrow. Nor the day after that, nor even the day after that. OK?'

Travis tapped his fingers on the mantlepiece while he listened.

McLeod touched my shoulder. 'How far d'ye reckon to get tomorrow?'

I listened to the buses on Whitehall and watched Travis. 'We'll have a rabbit. Then I'll show him a sample of grass. He thinks I'm a dealer in a syndicate or something. It's the only way to get close.'

Hamilton nodded at Travis.

'Michael?'

Travis straightened. 'Tomorrow we take Cohen.'

Hamilton swivelled in his chair and stared at the lights across the street. I leaned towards him.

'Hamilton?' He didn't seem to hear. 'Hamilton. You better tell him. He'll blow the whole trick.' Silence. I stood up. 'Hamilton. D'you hear me?'

McLeod shifted. 'Sit down.'

But I could see Cain's price twinkling through my fingers.

'Hamilton. Tell him.'

Hamilton turned and fumbled in his drawer. 'Explain, Michael.' He opened a packet of Rennies.

'Don't – '

McLeod's fingers bruised my arm.

Travis paced the lino. 'If we take Cohen tomorrow the film could be returned within hours. It could be done quietly.' He shoved his hands into his pockets, jacket flaring behind him. 'If Cohen hasn't actually got the film I promise you it won't take long to find who has. You know my view, Roger. You *must* strike first.' His eyes shone. Napoleon in a Savile Row suit.

'Crap,' I said. 'You . . . you d'nno the kind of opposition you're up against.' I belched. 'There's a bloke called Lacey croaking in the Royal Free this very bloody minute could tell you a thing or three about Cohen, by Christ . . .'

'Gordon?' Hamilton scribbled on his blotter.

'No.' McLeod looked tired. 'The timing's wrong.' Travis

loomed into the light.

'What?'

McLeod ground his fag into Hamilton's ashtray, one bloodshot eye cocked at Travis.

'I said the timing's wrong.'

'McLeod.' Travis put his hands on his hips. 'Is that your only reason?'

'It's better than most.'

Travis wheeled. 'Roger – ?'

'Mr Grant.' Hamilton straightened. 'You will meet Cohen as arranged.'

'And?' hissed Travis.

'We wait.' Hamilton pressed three fingers to his stomach. 'We wait for Mr Grant to locate the film.' Travis opened his mouth, thought better of it and paced over to the window. I relaxed. The room had slowed but my head ached something chronic.

'Fine. But don't expect nothing tomorrow. Don't expect anything for a coupla days. Say three days. I might get a sniff by then.'

'Three days. The nineteenth.'

'Don't remind me.' I climbed to my feet.

Travis turned his back while McLeod followed me to the door. 'Harry.' I turned. He shrugged. 'No matter. Get some shut-eye, eh?'

I used a smile. 'Confucius he say bloke that kip could lose his grip. I don't trust myself to wake up.'

McLeod was gunning for Travis.

'Ye're a survivor. I recognize the eyes.'

'Yeah. I use Brasso. What about you?'

On the way up Whitehall I passed a bloke with very fair hair.

Fifteen

The bed smelled like a rucksack on a route-march so at five in the morning I got up and sat in the armchair finishing what was left of the gin. Cain. Everything else rattled by like the dialogue in a foreign film, actors playing out a script written by the same monkey that could rewrite Genesis given enough time. Christ, if Lacey could lift a bracelet that easy I could, because Lacey was nowhere compared to H. Grant when it comes to the flash fingers.

And look what happened to Lacey.

I took my time having a shave and dressed careful in my suèdes on account of if you're well-dressed you feel better in yourself. Don't you? Well anyway, it made me feel almost normal and all I wanted for an hour was to kid myself I was just another blue-eyed berk with no more bother than the rental on the telly. At half-nine I stuffed Cheryl-Jo's grass in my pockets and drove to Regent's Park, leaving the motor on the inner ring. The day said summer soon. The sun was warming up the tree-trunks and bouncing off the dew while shadows broke and spread like ink-blots on the grass. The Parks Department coasted the lawns in motor-mowers that growled like boats on Sunday afternoon. The citizens had mostly gone to work so those on show were layabouts, nannies come slumming from Chester Terrace, slant-eyed girls on holiday, and retired bank managers reading the *Telegraph*. I doddled to the rose garden, not because I'm partial to roses or flowers in general but because it was quiet and let you think, disturbed only by the odd jet tearing the sky like canvas.

Six days.

I had a cup of coffee with a slice of toast in the tea-room, not the serve-yourself but the one where hens from Swiss Cottage haggle the price of cheesecake. I couldn't swallow so I sat on the terrace spraying crumbs to the pigeons. And I didn't like the way people were acting. An old geezer at a table was pretending to read a paper but every time I looked he was watching me, warm little worker tucked up snug, inspecting people like germs under a microscope. And the waitress leaned on the floor-length glass in the caff watching me feed the birds. I didn't leave a tip.

The main path through the park is about a mile long, running South and striped with the shadows of the trees that line the edges. It's so straight you can watch a person walk clear from one end to the other if you concentrate, but further off individuals all telescope into a mob so you lose your mark if you lift your eyes. I stood in the middle of the path wondering whether to walk up past the Zoo and round the outer circle to the car. A familiar head in the crowd, there, maybe a quarter-mile North, fair hair, blond. I started to walk. Clearer, fair hair, blond, tall, taller than the rest, trees like bars, bars on a cell, no way out, nearer, near. Close.

He was young. Maybe twenty. He didn't look as he passed.

I stared at the concrete. You had to laugh. I sat on a bench with my hands over my mouth to muffle the giggles because it seemed daft to think of a grown man chuckling to himself. When I looked at my watch it was coming on for noon so I strolled down the path to the Grenadier. A few tots of mother's warmed me up and I sat tucked in a corner watching a plumber eat a steak pie. About two I walked to the car.

Putney Bridge is down the bottom of the Fulham Palace Road and is where they start the boat race to Hammersmith every year I'm told. On the Fulham side you've got your red-brick shops and houses in such a jumble that the antique shops find themselves sharing an entrance with the butcher and there's a fallout from the bead-and-button groupies up the King's Road. But no self-respecting bass guitar would drop further than the junction, and South of the river just doesn't exist, which is a point of view I can understand. South-West of the bridge it's like a dock only the shipping is mostly dinghies and nothing to do with containers and Excise. It's a kind of yacht-basin with slipways and a paved frontage, the houses set back across the road parallel to the river – old houses with bow windows and curly balconies that shout Nigel loud as an Aston Martin. They say Sunday's the day for tailored jeans, a day for painting and splicing and polishing, birds in wellies being careful of their nails. Putney High Street runs at right angles to all this, away from the river, and Putney High Street is not Nigel country. In fact you need a passport to move from one to the other. The High Street is all Co-ops with 2p off and Odeons showing Elvis. Half the shoppers have never been up West in their lives, which makes it an unusual manor for a sauna.

The A-One used twenty feet of frontage glazed black so the herberts were left wishing they only had the bread. To clear all doubts about the merchandise the name was painted in sexy gold. Inside, your punter knew he'd get value for money; deep white pile and pink drapes over black glass, technicolor stills of chicks pressing cleavage on blokes sweating into linen while crimson nails played dreams on flab. The desk was faced with quilted pink. On one end stood a brass telephone two feet tall. That and a leather-bound appointment book were the only items decorating the teak. Apart from the receptionist's boobs. I wondered if the oil on her skin helped the customers or just made her difficult to catch.

'Good afternoon.' White teeth, cantilevered lashes. I leaned on the desk. 'I'd like . . . a sauna.'

'Do you have an appointment, sir?'

'No.'

Her hair stroked the pages. 'It's difficult without an appointment.'

'Well maybe I don't need the actual sauna. I mean, I've just got to meet somebody here.'

The eyes iced. 'We expect all our customers to enjoy the full therapy, sir.'

'Yeah. Well maybe I could sit in there and, you know, wait for him.'

'I'm afraid that won't be possible.'

'Look. If it's that much bother don't worry. I'll hang about outside.'

But she wasn't out front for nothing. 'One moment.' She lifted the brass ear-piece. 'Julie? Did you have a cancellation this afternoon . . . ? Yes, fine.' She waved her lashes. 'We can fit you in after all. May I have your name?'

'Smith.'

She was used to it. 'That will be . . . three pounds for the sauna and . . . five-fifty for the massage. Eight-fifty in all, inclusive of VAT.' Her teeth dazzled me. 'Tips at your discretion, sir.'

'Tips?'

'For your masseuse, sir.' She lifted her arms to adjust her hair while I held on to the edge of the desk. 'Her name is Julie. You'll like her.' She led me to a door. 'She'll be with you soon.'

I was stood in a room like a four-poster with the curtains drawn. Lime-green satin was pinched into the centre of the ceiling, falling in four sails to a scalloped fringe on the walls. Something like a hydrangea glowed and tinkled in one corner, every leaf and petal made of tinted glass. There were three easy chairs, one of them showing a pair of fat trousers hiding behind a motor magazine. I dropped into a seat and inspected the hydrangea while the party in fat trousers peered cautious over a picture of the new Jaguar. A bird came in wearing a clip-board and the briefest shorts this side of sincerity, flashing new moons of buttock when she turned.

'Mr Blackstock?' She lit the room with a smile. The joker in the chair dropped his magazine.

'Christine?' He stood. 'You remember me . . . ?'

'Of course.' She hadn't even looked at him. 'This way please.'

Mr Blackstock watched the new moons twinkle, sighed, and trotted after.

I'd sat back and closed my eyes when I heard the door. Julie was dressed like Christine but underneath the mascara she was a homely girl.

'Mr Smith?'

I followed her down a corridor lined with doors like two rows of teeth.

'Here. After you.'

A white-painted cubicle with a bed standing centre rear. A small table, a chair and a hanging rail. Julie shut the door, breathed a smile and dropped her clipboard on the chair.

'Is this your first visit, Mr Smith?'

'Right.'

She patted the bed. 'Take off your clothes and lie down, please.'

I hadn't got time. 'Look, all I want is the steam-room. D'you mind if . . .' Her shoulders slumped. 'What's up?'

'Nothing.'

'I haven't got . . . oh Christ.' I scratched my head. 'Look, don't . . .'

'You're the second today.'

'Don't take it personal, please.' I was getting a tenner out of my pocket. 'Why don't you just stop here for a bit? Nobody'll know the difference.'

She took the tenner. 'Where are you going?'

'The steam-room.' I opened the door. 'Hang about and you can show me out.'

'Your clothes.' She giggled behind the tenner. 'You can't go to the steam-room with your clothes on.'

'Bloody hell.'

'Wear this.' She passed a hand-towel.

I turned my back and slipped the packet of grass under the towel.

'See you.'

I could hear the pool before I got there. It was in a hall carved in tiles bold as jungle, wet, steamy and vivid, echoing the gulps of the man in the water as he heaved and plunged. I guessed most of the customers were busy bouncing their tenner's worth in the cubicles. I sat on a bench. He was fit, this swimmer, lithe and confident, and anyway I'd rather do business beside a pool than in a pressure-cooker. I knew I was right when a door opened and a figure broke through a cloud of white steam; it just wasn't healthy in there, you could tell because this guy had wrapped his head in a towel for protection. He stepped fast round the edge and out through the door to the corridor, couldn't wait to get away and I didn't blame him. The man in the water spread his hands on the tiles and heaved upright in one sweep, standing naked while he shook the water out of his hair. Then he turned. He was the same height and build but he wasn't Cohen. He walked towards me, clearing an ear with his finger. I stood up. He took a towel off the bench, nodded, rubbed his scalp and left by the opposite door.

It must've been three-twenty when I opened the door to the steam-room, coughing with shock. It was almost bearable if you crouched.

'Cohen?'

It was like saying goodbye at Euston before they discovered diesel. I took a step into the steam.

'Cohen?'

I couldn't see my hand at eighteen inches. Hot white steam scorched my lungs and bubbled on my skin.

'Cohen?'

My toe stubbed against a step, about a foot high, a terrace rising into the cloud, each level hotter than the last.

'Cohen.'

The moisture on the steps was pink. A hand dangled over the top step. I coughed and grabbed for his hair. It was Cohen all right but I shouldn't have moved his head.

I trailed pink down the steps, scrabbled at the door and into the hall while the pink seeped towards the pool. I plunged into the blue cool, wallowing and scouring, but pink rivulets poised at the edge and pooled on the surface like dye. I hauled myself out, snatched my towel and cut for the door. The pink dye was spreading on the water.

Julie was sitting on the bed.

'How d'you feel now?'

'Fine.'

She stroked my chest with the towel. 'You know . . .'

'Not now.'

'When you're ready.' She flung the towel on the bed and stood by the door, arms folded. I ran a comb through my hair, feeling the water dampen my collar. Julie caught my arm in the corridor.

'Are you from the *News of the World*?'

'Our reporter made an excuse and left.'

The bird in reception glanced up. 'Our card.' She flashed her teeth. 'I hope you enjoyed your visit?'

I took the card. 'Sauna Sex Scandal Shock Probe. See you in the comics.'

I was half-way down the High Street when I remembered the grass. I'd dropped it in the steam-room.

Sixteen

'Hamilton!'

He'd been dictating into a tape-recorder. Mike in one hand, eyebrows arched, he stared from me to his secretary.

'Sorry, Mr Hamilton.' She tried to push past. 'I told him you weren't . . .'

'Sod off,' I said.

Hamilton nodded. 'It's all right, Sheila.' He looked at his watch. 'Why don't you go home? It's turned five-thirty.' She slammed the door behind her.

'You're not playing Chief any more,' I told him. 'This is one puppet that won't be jerked again.'

He looked small and frightened as he wound the flex round the mike and stowed it in a drawer.

'Please . . . won't you sit down?'

'I'm not stopping. I came to tell you to get knotted. Fuck off. Goodnight.' I stepped to the door.

He stood, slight figure in the gloom of the window. 'Mr Grant. Won't you at least tell me . . .' he spread his palms, 'what has upset you?'

I opened the door. 'Oh, nothing. It's just I'm quick to take offence, that's all. It bothers me when the party I'm due to meet turns up with an extra mouth in his throat. But don't you pay no attention to me, Roger old son. I shan't be lurking round your orbit for centuries yet. Just forget you ever met me, OK? It'll be a pleasure to do the same for you.'

'Mr Grant.' Something about his voice brought me back into the room. 'Please sit down.'

I left the door open. 'And if you're still wondering, I mean Cohen. He's lost his tan.'

Hamilton got up and shut the door. 'Drink?'

'No. Yes.'

He poured scotch into a couple of glasses. 'When?'

'Before I got there.' I gulped and coughed. 'He was dead when I got there. OK? You tell Collinson that. He was dead when I got there.' I set the empty glass on the desk. 'I don't care a damn what you do now, Hamilton. Get Quist. Get Robert bloody Mark if you like. I'll take my chances. Even Brixton's better than this.'

I meant it. With six days to go. There had to be another way.

'Before you go . . .' Hamilton reached for his Rennies, 'where exactly was the body?'

'In the steam-room. He was dead when I got there.'

He dropped a tablet in his mouth. 'Did you, er, did you see anybody go into the steam-room before you?' He splashed whisky into my glass. 'Please think carefully. It's . . . important.'

'Don't you bloody tell me what's important. I was there. I'm involved.'

'Please. Was anybody there before you?'

I hadn't meant to drain the glass so quick. 'No.' A shape wrapped in a towel. 'Yes.'

'Who?'

I hollered. 'How the hell do I know?'

'Try to remember.' He was talking to the bookshelves again. 'Are you certain you, er, didn't recognize . . . the walk, say, or the build?'

In the silence that followed I listened to him breathe.

'You say that like . . .'

'Like . . . ?'

'Forget it.' I reached for the bottle. Hamilton knew who'd killed Cohen, and he suspected I'd recognized the killer. It had to be somebody we both knew.

'I'm . . . awfully sorry this has happened.'

I laughed too loud. 'Are you? Awfully?' Travis? McLeod?

'Mr Grant . . .'

'And I left the bloody grass there.' I ran a hand through my hair. 'Jesus Christ what a mess. Tell Collinson that too in case he gets ideas. I dropped the grass when I found Cohen. He was dead when I got there.'

Hamilton pressed his fingers together. 'What will you do now?'

'Get pissed.'

'I mean . . . what are your plans?'

'I see the Director of London Transport's retiring. I thought I might apply.' I shuddered on another mouthful. 'How the hell do I know? Anything, long as I don't have to roll my bloodshots on you and your lot again.'

He sighed. 'I did try to warn you.'

'Thanks.'

'We're dealing with . . . a dangerous man.'

'You are.'

'We.'

I knocked a glass with my elbow. 'Look. You don't seem to be hearing too good on top of everything else. What's the problem, ulcers gone to your ears?' I stabbed the desk with a finger. 'I resign. OK? You wanna turn me over? Fine. That's all right by me. But sweetheart like they say in the movies, we're through.' I stood, leaning heavy on the back of the chair. 'Good luck. And get a pro to referee your two monkeys otherwise they'll slaughter each other.'

'Will the police believe you, Mr Grant?'

I stopped. 'I'll take my chances, like I said.'

'That's not what I mean.' He'd lost his nervousness and that made me uneasy.

'What *do* you mean then?'

'The police will have found the . . . package you left in the steam-room.'

'You wouldn't.' I sat down slow.

'It would be . . . unfortunate if you . . . dropped out at this stage. I need you, Mr Grant. We're very near the end.'

'You wouldn't.'

Hamilton shrugged. 'After all, I've only your word. What am I to say when Collinson asks?'

I rolled an empty glass against my forehead. 'If I stay?'

'If you stay . . .' he took the glass and filled it, 'I'm sure I shall be able to persuade Jimmy Collinson that your story is true.'

'Hamilton. Don't ever turn your back on me.'

His expression bothered me. 'I hope you measure up to your threats, Mr Grant. We'll find out. Remember Cohen.' He straightened his shoulders. 'D'you have a gun?'

I splashed scotch on the desk.

'A gun?'

'I leave the thought with you. Meanwhile I expect you to find the film.'

'Look – '

'Find it.' He opened the door. 'Goodbye, Mr Grant.'

I bought two bottles of Gilbey's on the way home. Back in the gaff I slumped on the bed and poured a treble, ferrying the glass to my mouth in two hands. The phone started ringing but the journey wasn't worth the effort because I couldn't hear clearly when I got there.

'Who?' The Major. 'Not now, for Chrissake.'

'It's important, old man – '

'Yeah. Not now. I'll call you back, OK?'

I left the receiver squawking on the end of the cable. My glass was empty. I found the bottle beside the couch and sat on the floor to pour another. The rucks in the mat weren't so bad when you got used to them.

Fair hair exploded into white light. A corner, cold walls, unsteady feet.

'Mr Grant?'

I tried to open my eyes against handfuls of shrapnel.

'Mr Grant?'

A figure wavering near the door. I was standing in the corner of the gaff, arms crossed in front of my face.

'Mr Grant.' Bishop in an old dressing-gown. 'There's a visitor for you.'

'Who . . . ?' My throat burned.

'D'you think he's all right?' Bishop again.

'He's all right. Thank you.' I knew the voice but the slam of the door shut the name out.

'Sit down,' Her tone was cold.

'Well if it isn't the dizzy deb.' I groped for the bottle. 'Have a drink.'

The bottle fell, pumping spurts of gin on the mat. I stretched but she kicked the bottle across the room, gin spraying like a catherine wheel.

'Christ.' I shaded my eyes. 'That set me back three-fifty.'

'Get up.'

I rescued the bottle and pushed my head careful into the light. The walls moved so I held the back of the couch.

'Not much left but you're welcome . . .'

'Save it.'

She was dressed in jeans and an old grey sweater, hair in tails about her face, eyes puffed.

'You look . . . like a . . . boiled blanket.' I clutched the couch.

'I've just heard about Beau.'

'Beau.' I punched at my shirt-tail. ''Scuse my apparel, won't you?'

'Beau.'

'Beau.' Bits of the afternoon showered into my head like sparks. 'Hang about. I didn't have nothing to do with that.'

She smiled like cold water. 'No?'

'No.' I scraped my eyes. 'Somebody . . . somebody got there before me.'

'Of course.' Her face glistened. 'You haven't the courage to do it yourself. Who did you send?'

I slumped on the chair, hands dangling. 'Believe what you like.' I studied the gin bottle. 'You and Hamilton. You're two of a kind. You deserve each other. I'm looking out for me.'

Her hair stuck to her tears. 'It was you. It was Roger. What difference does it make who used the knife?'

'No.' I tried to pour a drink. 'Wasn't me. Wasn't Hamilton.'

I sucked fire and coughed till the room dimmed. 'It was Hamilton's mark.'

'Who?'

'The bloody mark. Ask Hamilton. Some party at the Bureau.' I drank. 'Hamilton's put the finger on a spy, and Beau nicked the evidence. The mark got to him first, that's all.'

'Don't lie to me.' Her eyes were raw.

'No evidence, no mark.' I swallowed. 'Simple.'

She pushed her face close. 'Don't imagine it's over. For what you've done . . . for what Roger did . . .' she sank to the arm of the couch.

'You won't.' I was tired. 'You won't do anything. I'll be in the nick. Or the river. And Hamilton's tougher than a horse's hoof. He'll be a sir or something. You won't get within a mile of him.'

'He's responsible.' She was on her feet, leaning over me. 'You're nothing. You're just currency in one of Roger's fucking games. You think the Fabergé's that important to him? Do you?'

I grabbed her shoulders. 'Not the Fabergé, you bitch!' Her hair whipped my face. 'The film. The bloody film! For Chrissake save us all the bother and say where it is!'

'Film?'

I shook her again. 'Tell!'

'What film?'

'Oh Jesus.' I let her go. 'You're really asking for it, you know?'

'What film?'

I tried to collect the strands wafting in my head. 'The film your mates nicked with the Fabergé.'

She started to shake her head.

'There was no film.' Her head moved faster. 'There was no film in the safe. *I was there.*'

I sat down.

'D'you see what I mean?' She wiped her face. 'D'you see what a fool he's made of you?' She started to laugh. 'Poor Willie. Did they tell you lies?' I couldn't tell whether she was laughing or crying.

'Go home.'

'Big Strong Willie.' She clucked. 'No. You couldn't have done that to Beau. Not you. But what about Roger? Roger pipes and Willie dances.' Her voice steadied. 'You'll remember Roger, won't you love? What did he tell you? What sort of film was it supposed to be?'

I listened to my voice. 'Thirty-five mill.'

'Oh my God.' She laughed.

'Shut it.'

'Sorry. It's just so funny. Shall I tell you what I've done? Shall I?' She sat beside me. 'Earlier tonight, after I heard about Beau . . .'

'Get out.'

'I will darling. But listen before I go.' She cupped her hands round my ear. 'I carried the Fabergé to Hungerford Bridge and threw it in the river.'

I shoved her off. 'What?'

'D'you like that, Willie?' She watched my fist clench. 'Why don't you? Hit me. Surely even you're capable of that? Try.'

I dragged her to the door. 'You'll get yours, sweetheart, I promise.'

She fell against the balustrade and I listened to her laughing all the way down the stairs.

I dragged my suitcase off the wardrobe and left it gaping on the bed, bundling shirts and jackets and ties as they came to hand. Sweat dripped off my nose. Without the chess set the only offer I had for Mister Cain was distance, the greater and sooner the better. Or was it? I watched the movements of my hands slow till they stopped. Then I sat down among the clothes on the bed.

When I looked at my watch it was four o'clock. The bottle-cap in my palm had left a red circle. I scooped the bottle from under the couch and screwed the top tight, set it on the table and rinsed the glass in the kitchen. My hands were steadier. I stood in the doorway looking at the shambles, then stepped over the mat to pick up the small table and straighten the cushions on the couch. I was moving faster. Then the bedclothes, sheets taut, blankets smooth, bed square in the corner. There was a pile of empties under the table which I collected and stored neat in the kitchen, then opened the window and let the night scour the smell of failure. I sipped a cup of Nescafé while grey seeped through the glass. A milk-float. Somebody shouting. By six I was shaved and clean.

The ten grand was there but it never had been the Fabergé. Ten thousand pounds was the price of an idea, a bit of fancy, a film invented by Hamilton to flush a spy. Travis or McLeod. Why else would Hamilton brief them both every step of the way? He wanted one of them and he was shaking him till his nerve cracked. Travis? Or McLeod? The beauty of it was that the trap wouldn't snap if the spy sussed the film for a fiction. And that meant yours truly, with his new-found knowledge, was ensconced in a unique and happy earning situation. I was going to sell a non-existent film.

I dressed in black slacks and pink shirt and hung my gear back in the wardrobe. Then I ate breakfast. At eight o'clock I called Hamilton at home.

'I've been thinking.'

'Yes?'

'I got a lead last night. Somebody came to see me.'

'Who?'

'I can't say right now.' I breathed deep. 'I think I know where the film is.'

A long pause.

'Mr Grant.' He spoke quietly. 'Remember. The man we're after has just murdered Cohen. He needs that film.'

'I'll mind out.'

One way or another Hamilton was going to pay, and the price of success was ten grand.

Five days.

Seventeen

I bought a dozen Cokes and five bags of crisps during the morning. Bishop caught me on the way back.

'Hope it was OK last night.' His eyebrows bounced meaningfully.

'What?'

'That girl.'

'Oh her. Yeah, she's all right. Ta.'

He took me aside. 'Took one look and said to myself, she's in trouble. You can tell. Sorted out, was it?'

'She's OK now. Thanks for letting her in.'

I climbed the stairs and settled in for the day, pouring Coke like itchy water down my throat and getting rid of the taste with the crisps, which left me thirsty.

I was going to sell a non-existent film.

If I offered the film to Hamilton direct he'd laugh in my face. Travis and McLeod. As an outsider there was no way I could figure which of them was Hamilton's mark. They both showed keen to get the film and that meant one of them knew the truth and was helping Hamilton shake the tree. So my earning power hinged on Hamilton knowing the mark had seen me offer the film for sale, which meant the offer had to be made twice, once through Travis and once through McLeod. Only one of them would pass it on, but Hamilton had to assume I'd told both and if he didn't cough up he was blown. It took a long time to figure through, and it was midnight when I finally turned in.

I started early.

'What is it?' Travis was curt.

'Is anybody with you?'

'No.'

'I gotta see you.' I tapped the coin-box. 'Alone.'

Like a good officer, he made quick decisions. 'Meet me at the Kew River Club. Six-thirty.'

'Where?'

He spoke through his teeth. 'The Kew River Club.'

'I hear you. Where is it?'

'East of Strand-on-the Green, about a hundred yards.' Somebody must've come into his office. 'Ask for me there.' He dropped the phone before I could answer.

There's a riverside walk off Strand-on-the-Green, lined by old cottages facing the river and showing foot-high water-barriers. It's like Bangladesh when the river floods only you don't need helicopters to fish the citizens out because most have got their own boats and those that haven't float downstream on their Rembrandts. There are gaps between the cottages but the new houses are so careful you don't notice the difference. The City Barge, beside the walk, used to pour malt into the bargees but now dribbles Martini on Hawaiian shirts most of the year. The Kew River Club is at the end of the path, a glass cube on stilts at a bend in the river where the members sink pink gins and watch their mates sweat into the water. Boat-sheds poise on slipways each side of the clubhouse showing masts and rigging thick as a forest. You can fall in the Thames these days without getting nicked by the clinic but there was a time when you'd catch something nastier than a bad dose of mackerel. The path petered out to shingle and I realized you didn't have to walk the tow-path to get there. The Jags and Bentleys parked on the gravel at the back.

There were a couple or three boats heeling about, sails dipping into the green while the yachtsmen leaned like commandos on a cliff. The odd bloke was painting or scrubbing his boat on the slipway and the sheds were crowded with chat and laughter. It smells clean at Chiswick, like new rain in a puddle, and there's not the kind of rubbish that washes up at Limehouse. I picked over the slipways and took the wooden steps two at a time. The view was handsome, right up to Kew Bridge on one side. The opposite bank was overgrown, willows trailing fingers in the current and showing roots like men with no boots. I pushed through a pair of glass doors into a big airy room, not like a boozer really but there was a bar at the back, most of the space being taken up by low tables and easy chairs. The windows were laid out so you could put your feet up and watch the race on the river. The walls were plastered by plates and shields and trophies that would've fetched a bundle as a job lot but that wasn't why I was here. There was a thin party in shirt-sleeves behind the bar and since he was the nearest representation of life in the place I called out.

'Mr Travis here yet?'

'Are you a member?'

'I'm looking for a mate of mine.' I watched his marbles scan the cut of my blazer. 'Michael Travis. He's a member.' He folded his cloth, ducked under the bar and pointed at a boat slicing downstream, eight oars chopping as one. The sun was setting on Kew Bridge and the whole picture was very tasty.

'There's Mr Travis. Second from the bows.'

The boat skimmed out of range while he spoke.

'Thanks.' I sat on a window-bench.

Without a membership card it was clear I wasn't due a glass of water, and if asked for a forecast on the basis of perceptible vibes just then I would've estimated my chances of membership as approximately nowhere. So I stepped out to the verandah and clumped down the steps to wait on the shingle. The boat was back in ten minutes, oars heaving while the guv'nor chanted like Geronimo praying for rain. They were level with the club-house when his voice changed, and, like magic, the oars poised still as a swan gliding home. The guv'nor worked a little rudder and the nose aimed for the beach, slowing. The crew climbed into the water, healthy chaps, blue shorts and brown muscles. The boat dripped as they lifted, pointed at the sheds and began to trot up the shingle. Travis, second from the front, dropped a curt nod. His face was red and he looked younger than he did in his three-ton suit. I followed, careful not to cut my shoes on the stones.

Five minutes later they trickled out in groups of two or three. Travis, zipped up in a track suit with a towel round his neck, was having a rabbit with the guv'nor, who was running his finger down a page on a clip-board. Travis rummaged in a duffle-bag and pulled out his specs-case, setting a pair of glasses careful on his nose to read the list. Then he slapped the guv'nor on the shoulder and walked to me.

'I have to change. Come upstairs.'

I followed him up the steps. A couple of people were sat at a table in the club-room, and Travis waved and smiled. The barman was grinning.

'Most enjoyable, Mr Travis. I watched from the window.'

'Thanks, Freddie. Set 'em up while I change, will you? A scotch-and-soda for me and . . .'

'A ginger ale.'

Travis shouldered his bag and pushed through a door at the back. I climbed on a barstool and watched Freddie.

'Not too busy this evening, then?' He ignored me. 'Part time, is it?'

'How, sir?' He had bother getting the words through his teeth but I know Poplar when I hear it.

'The job.'

He dropped the glasses on the counter. 'Sir.'

'Call me Harry.'

'That'll be seventy-five.'

'Michael's account.'

He glanced over his shoulder. 'We don't like your type here.'

'We don't like being here. Who dragged you up-river?'

I carried the drinks to the window and waited for Travis. He looked clean, glowing face above a crew neck sweater and a cravat folded careful at his throat. He stopped for a word with his mates at the table near the bar while I sussed the cavalry twills and the heavy waves of his hair. He sat down, back to the glass.

I raised my drink. 'HM Queen.'

It was like drinking in a greenhouse. The sun had almost gone, leaving the room in a flush. Travis found a pipe and a pouch in his pocket. The pipe was red and shiny and he filled the bowl like a man who has to concentrate. It took four matches to get it going. He looked like an ad for Brut.

'Thought I heard you say something about Burnham last time?' I asked.

He watched the river. 'I keep a trimaran there.'

'Look.' I sipped my ginger ale. 'Sorry to bother you like this, only something's come up. I dunno whether I'm doing the right thing, but, anyway, I thought you might be interested.'

'Why me?'

I looked surprised. 'I should've thought that was obvious.'

'What do you want?' He tried to talk past the stem of his pipe.

'You heard about Cohen?'

'Is that what you came to ask me?'

'It wasn't me, you know.'

He snorted. 'Is that an apology?'

'I don't like being used for bait.'

'Nobody asked whether you liked it.' Like the pipe, his words were big and manly. 'Look, Grant, if that was all you wanted to say I needn't keep you longer.'

I spoke towards the floor. 'You could make it easier for me. Gimme a chance. Tell me who it is.'

Somebody switched on the lights and room changed from a goldfish bowl to a hall of mirrors. I watched Travis in the glass.

'You know too much already. You would have been more effective blind.'

'Must get up your nose, that, having bad decisions made

over your head.' I took a sip of fizz. 'Why d'you put up with it?'

He watched me till I looked away. 'You're a curious mixture. Ignorance and confidence. You could do with less of both.'

'Tell me who it is.'

He finished his drink. 'You came to tell me something.'

'I know where the film is.'

The muscles in his face tensed.

'Where?'

'Uh-uh.' I wagged a finger. 'You're the hit-'em-where-it-hurts merchant, right? If I tell you you'll bust the whole thing. Anyway it's not as easy as that.'

'Where is it?'

'Bloke I met. Mate of Cohen's.'

'Where is it?'

'It was a doddle for him after Cohen got hit. You might say Hamilton's mark did us all a favour. But like I said, it's not as easy for us.' I was starting to enjoy myself. 'I mean, what would you do? This geezer, this mate of Cohen's, all his life he's fancied a Rolls and a little place by the sea somewhere. St Trop, more than likely. This might be his last chance.'

Travis leaned against the window. 'Very astute of him.'

'You know you're really very sharp? So sharp I reckon I'll buy you a drink.'

I liked snapping my fingers at Freddie. 'A ginger ale and a scotch and soda for my friend here.' I didn't grant Freddie the benefit of a full-frontal scan because he didn't deserve it and anyway my happiness might've blinded him. I turned to Travis. 'The film's safe. And – no offence to present company – it's no good any interested party hitting me for it. I die like anybody else would you believe, but Sweetheart if I die this feller just disappears. OK?'

'How much?' Travis showed his hate.

'Ten grand.'

He searched my face for the funny bit. 'As I said. Ignorance and confidence.'

'Excuse me, Mr Travis baby, I thought I'd explained it isn't me.'

I thought Travis would crush the glass in his hands. 'And you seriously believe Roger Hamilton will swallow your story?'

I'd have died laughing but lucky for me old Freddie arrived with the booze. I dropped a oncer on the tray and left him two pee out of the change.

'Get hip, Travis. Don't you know I'm in enough trouble already? D'you think I'm that daft? Jesus Christ, let me tell you, I shall be double chuffed to wave goodbye with my arms in the right places. All I want out of this is out.'

'Hamilton will watch you fry before he pays out money like that. So will I.'

'That makes two, right?'

'Don't waste my time.'

'It'd be a pity, though, wouldn't it? He's a winner, this bloke with the film. He won't let go without the film, so you get empty nets and I get Death Row.' I shuddered on the ginger ale. 'Sleep on this: this joker with the film – he needs the gelt so bad he might even sell to somebody else. Some other interested party, know what I mean? It's up for grabs, Travis, you better face it.'

'Ignorance and confidence. And audacity.'

I sighed. 'I've already said. The money's not for me. Wish it was. Impecuniosity's an on-going problem with me.'

'I see no possibility of relief for you.' He caught my eye. 'Go to hell.'

'Ask Hamilton.'

'I think,' said Travis, 'I've heard enough.'

'Tell him it's his only chance. No gelt, no film. He can carve me for beef on Sunday if he wants, it won't do any good. I haven't got the film.'

'I find you fascinating.'

'You'll have to wait your turn. The fan club's already bulging.'

He studied the shine on his pipe. 'For instance, even if you'd got the money how could you possibly hold it?'

I yawned. 'Not boring you am I? Holding the money is not my problem. I'm not selling the film.'

'Of course.'

'But if I was I'd say Hamilton had no choice, wouldn't I?'

'Would you?'

I thought. 'See, I don't reckon you carry much weight in that manor, no offence, but it'd take more'n you to persuade him against.' He sneered but his fingers had tightened on his glass. 'You know him better than I do.' I shrugged, dead cool. 'Nice feller. A bit . . . pliable, though. Am I right? Maybe it's his ulcer.'

Travis picked up his duffle-bag.

'I see you're finished.' He drained his glass and dropped his pipe in his pocket. The group near the bar waved good-bye. I followed him down the wooden steps.

'Ask him.'

He ignored me. In the car-park he unlocked a silver Jensen and chucked his bag in the back. The three-ton suit swung on a hanger near his head.

'Nice piece of jam-jar.' I patted the paintwork.

He slammed the door and kicked the engine into a growl.

I said again: 'Ask him.'

The Jensen reversed in a wide circle and pulled away in a shower of gravel. I stood and listened to him burning up the road, then walked back down the tow-path and collected the 1300.

Eighteen

Finding McLeod would've foxed the Law on account of there being a hundred of him in the book and ten of those Gordons. Course, the Law would've nicked the lot and saved the questions but I struck lucky on round three. He lived in Islington and was that chuffed to hear my basso I thought he'd mistook me for his brother Bill from Banff. Anyway, I rolled the wheels to Castle Street about nine and was stunned to find he lived in a council estate. One of your moderns, all burnt brick and endless balconies framing a courtyard that lashed the garbage up the walls. Straight up, you had to bend down and shut your eyes to get across. Bits of trees stood raw in the lamplight and the builder had left a pile of concrete rings in one corner. There were maybe fifteen kids hung like grapes on the concrete shedding skin on the aggregate and snot on the paving. Slogans daubed the walls where the light let you see them and the kids dinned like Mons and Stalingrad sharing the evening between them. Tomorrow's Dillingers.

McLeod lived in a first-floor maisonette, the ground being reserved for the elderly so they got the beer cans first. I rang the bell and watched the kids murder each other below. A boy aged twelve opened the door, all arms and legs and hair hiding the spots on his face.

'Dad about?'

Hands on hips. 'Who wants him?'

'Say Harry.'

He shut the door so I rang again. There was a fight in the hall and McLeod looked out.

'Sorry. Come in.' He hollered down the passage. 'Colin! I'll not tell you again. Ye're not to shut the door on visitors!' The boy whined somewhere in the gaff. 'Enough of y'r lip, laddie, or I'll whip the skin off y'r backside.' He grinned. 'Bloody menace.' He pushed me along the passage, picking up a wet towel on the way. 'Kids are all disappointing. Ye can only do y'r best.'

'Give him time.' It wasn't what I meant but I said it anyway.

McLeod let me into the lounge. It was like stepping onto the terraces on Cup Final day. The telly crouched in a corner fusing its innards over the evening's action at Everton or somewhere, blasting commentary like some crazed auctioneer while little white figures weaved against the green. The boy hunched on a stool near the screen, biting his fingernails and spitting the bits on the mat. The remains of dinner littered the table, cold stew by the look of it, and every surface was strewn with books, magazines and old newspapers. A pile of dirty clothes climbed one corner and it was nearly a minute before I saw the nipper sitting among her books on the couch. She was about three and colouring like a con hacking through brick, tongue against her top lip, oblivious to everything.

McLeod bellowed. 'Turn it down!'

The boy was glued. 'Dad . . .' It was like the start of an air-raid warning. McLeod laid one on the side of the boy's head, not too hard. The boy lowered the volume so that you might just hear the fuzz-bells if you were expecting them. A woman came in and started to clear the table. She was about twenty years younger than McLeod but you could say she'd given up sooner than most. She was thin, wrapped in a quilted house-coat, bare legs, and her hair hung in strands about her cheek-bones. McLeod got between us.

'Harry Grant. My wife, Alice.'

Alice nodded. 'I wish you'd let me know when your friends are coming. I'm sure Mr Grant isn't used to visiting pigsties.'

I laughed. 'You know what they say. Family laughter, dustpans after.'

She bundled the tablecloth under her arm and sniffed. 'There's not much laughter in this house.'

'Drink?' McLeod fought for the sideboard, sweeping a load of wooden blocks to the floor as Alice left.

'No thanks.'

He waved a bottle. 'This'll change your mind.'

'No.'

He lifted shaggy eyebrows, shrugged, and poured one for himself.

'Sit down, Harry. It's good to see ye.' He pulled a pair of dolls off a chair. It smelled of cats. McLeod folded a colouring book and plumped into the couch beside the girl. 'Cheers.' He wiped his mouth. 'I hear ye'd a shock with friend Cohen?'

I nodded at the boy. 'Er . . .'

'Colin.' McLeod kicked the leg of the stool. 'Outside.'

'Dad . . .'

'Do as I say!'

The boy kicked the couch and slammed the door behind him. McLeod stretched a hand to lower the volume, leaving midgets miming on the green.

'Yeah. Your anonymous friend got there first.'

'Hamilton warned you. This laddie's getting desperate. If he cannot get the film himself he'll do anything to stop others getting it.'

'Thanks.'

'We'd not have got this far without ye.'

'Thanks again.'

'It's the truth.'

I watched the kid scrubbing the paper. 'Well this time he left the door open. Carving Cohen was the best break he's given me.'

'How's that?'

'Now I know where the film is.'

Mcleod rested his glass on the stains of his sweater. 'Where?'

'That would be telling.'

'Just so. Where?'

'Safe. For the time being.'

The girl dropped her books and climbed into McLeod's lap. He was gentle, holding her with one hand while he lifted his drink out of reach.

'I'll not need to remind ye . . .' he stroked the kid's hair, 'the last part of y'r task was delivery. We can help.'

'Yeah. And screw up the whole process. This is a caper requiring . . . tact.' I lit a cigar. 'It's me that's strapped to the cannon, boyo, and that gives me the right to do it my way.'

'And? What's your way? Ye'll not have come here without a proposition, will ye?'

'Are all Scotchmen bright as you?'

He kissed the girl's forehead. 'Who's a tired wee girl, then? We understand the English. We have the advantage of their xenophobia.'

'I dunno about xenophobia,' I told him, 'it's intuition keeps me going.'

'Is that what ye call it?' He laughed. 'Pass the bottle, Harry. Sure ye won't join me?'

I shook my head. 'I'm sure. Call it what you like.'

'How about compulsive maleficence?'

'Don't polish your morals for me buddy. I was chosen because I'm bent, remember?' I watched him pour with one hand. 'And what's so tidy about you? Christ I'd like a fiver for every time you and that pair of Tories have pulled the trigger. Civil little servants, conning the mugs by day and kissing the kids by night. You know the difference between you and me? I'll tell you. I wear one hat.'

He sipped. 'I do my job.'

'Maybe they'll give you a medal.'

'Where's the film?'

I crossed my legs. 'Well, there's a spot of bother surrounding this film. The party that knows of its whereabouts won't deliver until such time as a certain wad of readies is slapped in his hot and sweaty.'

McLeod grinned. 'Naturally. How much?'

'Would you believe ten thousand?'

He threw back his hair and roared a laugh, mouth so wide

you could've parked a bus between his teeth. Then he wiped his eyes.

'Harry, I love you.'

'Sugar, it's mutual.'

He straightened his sweater. 'I know you better than you think. Ye're not the only chancer making a bad start good.'

'I didn't . . .'

'I'd grown up in the Gorbals by the time you were born. D'ye know that that means?'

'It – '

'I know each bend in your brain.' The girl snuggled against his chest. 'It takes people differently.'

'Sure. You grew up superior. A con with a conscience.' The child fell into the cushions as he sat up.

'Aye. A conscience.' His face was flushed but maybe it was the whisky. The girl started to wail and McLeod knelt beside the couch mouthing words. Then he stood, the child tight to his chest. 'Aye. I've a conscience. And I've a duty.' The girl quietened.

'Funny.' I shook my head. 'You. Travis. Hamilton. D'you choose your mates or do they choose you?'

He sat, cradling the child. 'Happy coincidence.' He moved the baby and took a long swallow of whisky.

'Ever feel left out of things?'

'Left out?' He was drinking too fast. 'Because I'm a Celt? Tell me, what've you got in common with a lad like Travis? Ye're both English.' He messed his hair. 'Both Londoners.'

'You know what I mean.'

'Aye I do. And I'll tell you this. Travis and I have one major characteristic in common. Guilt. Him, for his money, his education, and for his privilege. Me for . . . different reasons.' He drank. 'It drives him to rash decisions.'

'And you to drink.'

He hadn't heard. 'He'll bear the scars all his life.'

I cleared my throat. 'About this gelt.'

'A fair try.'

'It really hurts me to hear you going on like that.'

'What a risk.' He shook his head. 'Ye cannot be that big a fool.'

'How d'you mean? '

'Just remember Cohen.'

'How could I ever forget?'

'And then,' he shoved a cushion under the child's head, 'remember Hamilton, Travis and me. The film is very important to all of us.'

I was suddenly talking fast. 'You need me, Honeychild, let's be clear about that. You need me alive and well and walking up Whitehall otherwise no film.'

He shrugged. 'We're pragmatists. Results are what count.'

'Right. And without me you get nowhere.'

'Have ye ever been so important before?' He poured another drink.

'Never. And I like it. But you've got me wrong.'

'Aye. The money's not for you.'

'Ask Hamilton.'

He swilled his glass. 'Why d' the English not drink?'

'It clouds the xenophobia.' He walked me into the passage.

'I like you, Harry.'

'Sure. Even if you've gotta drop me in the river.'

'Even that.' He opened the front door.

'Remember,' I said, 'no Harry no film, baby.'

'I remember.' He yawned. 'Baby.'

I was almost grinning when I dodged the Dillingers in the courtyard. McLeod and Travis had both heard the offer and I could've felt sorry for Hamilton. He'd spent months playing his catch like a sprat on a line when all of a sudden the berk he was using for bait starts working a wrinkle. So here was Roger Hamilton, stuck with a tap for ten grand and if he ignored it the sprat would suss him and the film for a con before you could cough Nikita Khrushchev. Any way you looked at it there was ten thousand nicker twinkling at the end of the rainbow. But for that kind of loot I'd gotta serve Hamilton's sprat on a plate. If I scarpered I'd get lead in the stomach with kippers come breakfast on Monday. Like the bloke on the gibbet said, all I need is time; time to pay Cain before Hamilton snatched back the bread. But the thought wiping my face straight was that the sprat wanted that film bad enough to try for it first, and that would suit Hamilton. No gratuities, and even the sprat couldn't stay hid after that.

Three days to go.

Nineteen

The bait had to look right. There had, for instance, to be a film. And a venue. It looked like that bit of the action was down to me, which was why I spent most of Friday looking for a site. A quiet spot on account of the leading man was that shy he wouldn't play to a full house. But then I had myself to worry about. If the stage was that isolated any one of the players might decide it would be best if Harry G just disappeared. So I wanted a cul-de-sac with an escape hatch. I was tangled in the traffic near London Bridge when I sussed perfection. Bankside.

Visiting Bankside and Southwark used to be like going up West only that was centuries before they invented Greek Street. I mean, the only reason for rolling through Ludgate in those days was to spend Sunday with the wife and kids watching the villains get topped at Tyburn, and even that had its limitations. So for real fuse-pops you nipped over London Bridge to where a brass cost a farthing, where the mob stoned actors, and where you could drop a guinea on a bear getting ripped by dogs. The Entertainment Centre of the World, was Bankside. There was even a time when the straights in the City shut the bridge for fear of contamination, and they weren't just thinking of the pox. The riverside was built dense on account of the mud on the roads which was four feet deep and dirtied the carpets – boozers, play-houses, warehouses and knock-shops spreading South. Then when the West End got fashionable the entertainment drifted North, leaving Southwark with its cathedral, a few bits of theatre, and a shore lined with landing stages. Trade took over, and Bankside mushroomed into the biggest loading depot West of the Pool. By the nineteenth century it was cluttered with warehouses in a thick ribbon. The demand for space forced the buildings high and the streets narrow. It must've been a very active manor. Trade slumped with railway haulage, and today the district stands derelict. The price of land being what it is you can't let capital like that earn birdseed so in the late sixties the bulldozers started ironing out the acres. There are still pockets left untouched, though.

Once you're in the maze it's like a film set for Jack the Ripper and I don't mean Herbert Lom. The walls block the sky, the tyres rumble on the cobbles, and the sniff of spice conjures shades of boozed-up matelots lurching after rum and tarts. The cobbles are littered with busted boxes and slates fallen off the roofs, so I parked the car and walked, checking my back for the echo of my footsteps. The last street was twelve feet wide, a stony channel parallel to the river, and if I'd sussed right the buildings backed onto the water. Further down a knife of sun cut the dust, lighting the pavement near a gap in the terrace. The gates still read 'Cooper's Yard'. I squeezed between them. The brickwork soared eighty feet both sides, framing an aching-bright keyhole view of the North bank. I picked over the setts, watching the frieze unfold. The drop to the river was thirty feet, unprotected apart from three capstans ground like apple-cores. I say river, but the water was twenty yards out, peeled back over gravel, tins and tyres. You could see from Tower Bridge to the Savoy, a panorama crowned by St Paul's pointing clean in the sun. If you didn't know what went on over there you might've described it as handsome, but thoughts like that are best left to swedes and Buddhists. My exit was one-way and I'd be a mile downstream in the dark before they realized I'd gone over. The yard had been a loading depot shared by two firms, and both buildings showed columns of double doors one above the other, capped by gantries. Every window was smashed but barred to deter the villains and the gates were the only way in. I rooted about and found the lid of an old packing-case which I dragged to the edge. I lit a cigar, brushing my hands while the smoke drifted in the light. It would do.

Bishop tried to tell me something as I mounted the stairs.

'Not now.' I pushed him off.

The door to the gaff was ajar. Being familiar with the modus operandi of your average tea-leaf I am particular about means of ingress, which is to say I'd left the bloody door locked. I stood fixed to the stairs while the door swung open.

Quist's mouth was twisted round a fag.

'You look worse every time I see you. Come in and put your feet up.'

He stepped aside while I fought for words.

'What brings the cavalry round my unworthy manor of a Friday?'

Quist sat on the arm of a chair and sent a jet of smoke towards the ceiling.

'Just a natter. Thought you might offer me a cuppa tea.'

'Piss off.'

He drummed his heel on the side of the chair.

'Harry. That's no way to treat a partner.'

'What d'you want?'

'S'pose partner's the wrong word really.' He patted the hair on his scalp, eyes pale. 'Colleague, more like. After all, we're both working for . . .'

My gut rose. 'I told you. He'll get the bread. Now get out.'

Quist was laughing, silent, tongue against his teeth.

'I can see you don't wanna be disturbed.' He wiped his mouth on his sleeve. 'Gotta lot to do, haven't you? Three days, Harry. Three days.' He stood up and butted his fag in the ashtray. 'Screw it up and I swear you'll die twice so help me.'

The door closed quiet behind him.

I fell on the bed like a sack of spuds, the sweat going cold under my arms. A knock.

I bust like plate glass: *'Who is it?'*

Bishop looked hurt. 'Only me.' He came in awkward. 'That chap. He said he was a friend of yours. So I let him in.' He frowned. 'Are you all right?'

'Just let me be.'

I listened to him go, then snatched the bottle off the sideboard. The mouth was poised over a glass when I caught a sniff and poured it down the sink. My head was clearing and it better stay that way.

By five I was calm enough to phone the PLA. They gave me high tides for Saturday and Sunday, there being no point bothering with high tides or hopes if I hadn't got the gelt by then. I sat down and worked out the moves step by step till my eyes felt like gnawed peaches and my head ached. I was going out for more Cokes when Bishop came heaving up the stairs. He was followed by Travis.

'Another visitor.' Bishop's eyebrows lifted. 'Do me a favour. Arrange to meet them downstairs.'

Travis looked immaculate in a dark blue suit and white shirt, carrying a briefcase and an umbrella.

'Slumming, Travis?'

'Open the door.'

'I haven't got much time.' I unlocked. 'I've promised to give a one-man show at the Scrubs tonight and I don't wanna be late.'

He opened his case. 'The money.'

What do you say when the axe bites the wood beside your head?

'Fancy a snort?'

He dropped a parcel on the table. 'Count it.'

'Anyway, I haven't got no booze. D'you believe I poured it down the sink?'

I turned my back so he wouldn't see my fingers chatter. It was all there in crisp new twenties.

'Well?'

I cleared my throat. 'Thank you to Her Majesty.'

'You're lucky, Grant.' Travis stood with feet apart, a guardsman at ease.

'Runs in the family,' I said. 'Told you he'd come through if you asked, didn't I?'

He snapped his briefcase. 'When and where?'

'Have a cuppa coffee?'

'Grant – '

'OK, OK. I'm supposed to phone this bloke tomorrow and tell him it's on or off. I'll be meeting him about eight. D'you know . . . er, Bankside?' I frowned. 'It's on my way home.'

'Bankside. Where?'

'I know a quiet place called Cooper's Yard, next to the river, off Tooley Street.'

He scribbled on his cheque book. 'What time?'

'Say . . . nine o'clock.'

The river would be fast and full by then.

'If you mention . . .'

I waved him quiet. 'I know. Think I'm stupid enough to derail the gravy train, Travis?'

He didn't say goodbye.

It took a while to get my hands steady enough to call the nick at Edgware Road. They couldn't find Quist, and the old panic started punching holes in my chest.

'Whaddaya mean, can't find him? Is this the nick or not? For Chrissake call him!'

The voice was cool. 'Urgent, is it, chum?'

'Urgent? Where is he?'

'Out on a case.'

'Where?'

'Who's speaking?'

'Look.' I took a long breath. 'When he comes in tell him Harry called. He'll know what it's about.'

I rang off before the questions got personal.

I popped a Coke and had a ponder. Like I'd figured, only one of Hamilton's boys had passed my offer on to his guv'nor.

Travis. That meant Travis was in the clear, Travis was the one helping Hamilton to flush the spy, McLeod. By making quick with the quiddies, Hamilton showed he knew I'd also told McLeod about the film, and it couldn't have been difficult to make sure McLeod heard I was collecting as per invoice. What McLeod didn't know was when and where, and there was no way Hamilton could tell him without blowing cover. So that part of it was down to me. Meantime Travis had been sent into the front line with me, and when we met at Bankside we'd be the bait in a trap designed for McLeod.

I only hoped Hamilton had brains enough to bring a regiment on the night. I collected some change and called McLeod.

'OK. It's quitting time. I can't get hold of Hamilton so I'm telling you. You got the film.'

I heard the baby whining. 'I'm glad ye've seen sense.' He waited. 'When can we meet?'

'I'm collecting tomorrow at eight. Say . . . nine?'

'Good. Where?'

'Cooper's Yard, Bankside. Off Tooley Street.'

A long pause. It must've sounded like a set-up but he'd got no choice.

'Why, for God's sake?'

'On account of I don't trust you or Hamilton any further than I can transport London Bridge. And because that particular manor will give good quiet cover for one or two mates of mine who are not altogether unfamiliar with the weight of shooters in their hands should anything be untoward. Tell Hamilton that too.'

'Laddie. All we want is the film.'

'Just remember I got fire-power.' I wished it was true.

'I will, I will.'

'You'll tell Hamilton?' I had to make it sound right.

'See ye there.'

If I was McLeod I wouldn't bother. I'd just plug the source like I'd done with Cohen. So I had to hold him off till the meeting and my only chance was to stay out of sight between now and then.

The gelt.

If Quist stayed shy the bundle had to stay out of Hamilton's reach but available for Cain. I called the nick again but Quist was still out. After a bit of a ponder I stuffed Travis's parcel under the shirts in the drawer, locked the gaff and wandered up Charlotte Street to the 1300. The spare wheel slots in a hollow under the mat in the boot. I heaved it out, collected the tyre wrenches, and wheeled it down the pavement. Bishop was shutting up shop.

'Hullo, Mr Grant. Flat tyre?' He held the front door open.

'Slow leak,' I told him. 'Don't mind me using the gaff, do you?'

'Rather you . . .'

'No mess,' I said, cheerful. 'Don't fret.'

Inside the gaff I laid the wheel on newspapers and let the air out of the valve with a matchstick. The tube came out easy once I'd loosened the tyre. The gelt was in twenties, ten bundles of a thousand nicker each, and though it was a shame to dirty the crispy lovelies I reckoned Cain wouldn't kill for the sake of a drop of axle-grease. The bread fitted snug between the rim and the tyre. After a wash I dressed in a pair of old cords and a windcheater. I mean, I didn't want to donate my best suèdes to Father Thames, did I? Within five minutes the spare was back in the boot and yours truly was steering the 1300 towards Leicester Square.

The traffic was snarled all the way into Charing Cross Road and back again with swedes daft enough to think they could find parking and berks collecting birds outside the Odeon and the Warner. I parked the motor careful on the double yellows, blocking three cars outside the Kentucky Pancake House, locked up and doddled off up the Sunroom. I'd earned a drink.

I saw nobody I knew except the spade and the usual layabouts slugging the ivory up the baize so I bought myself a tot and sat on the benches with my back to the wall, unravelling thoughts. Hamilton. Suppose he thought I'd scarpered with the bread? I tucked myself in the phone booth and stood the tot on a pile of directories. He sounded nervy. 'I've been trying to call you. Where are you?'

'Tell you where I'm not if you like.'

'I have your message. About tomorrow – '

'Just bring an army, OK?'

'That won't be possible.'

'Then bring your mate Collinson.'

'No.' He sounded shagged out. 'I'm sorry. You'll have to carry the meeting alone for a while.'

'What?' I knocked my glass off the books. 'Go to hell. I'm not showing without protection, no way, you better think again.'

'That's why I wanted to speak to you. You . . . know what to expect?'

I cussed blue. 'You've fitted up your bloke for the biggest con since Christ and I'm the berk out front. No chance. I won't do it without a shield.'

'He must be intercepted in the act, d'you see? Are you there? Mr Grant?'

'I resign.'

'Don't force me to . . .' he coughed. 'Please don't think I'm not grateful for the risks you've taken.'

'Thanks.'

'We're . . . acutely aware of your situation.'

'Good. Me too.'

'And we shall supply the only protection possible.'

'Which is?' I was snarling.

'A gun.'

'Jesus.'

He waited. 'Where are you, Mr Grant?'

'The Sunroom.' I listened to myself say it. 'Old Compton Street.'

'Thank you.'

I caught a touch of the ice-picks down the back. 'Wait a minute. I just wanna tell you this place is crowded, lots of pals of mine, and I won't be stopping long. Get me?'

'Wait there.'

'Maybe.'

'And . . .'

'What?'

'I'm happy that you reconsidered your position.'

I settled down against the wall.

At eleven the spade shook my shoulder.

'Harry Grant?' He jerked a thumb. 'Somebody want you.' I picked my way round the tables, stopping in the shade just in case. The feller at the door wore a cabbie's badge and carried a parcel under his arm.

'Package for you.'

It was a heavy box wrapped in brown paper. I carried it into the carsie for a peep. It was a .38 Smith and Wesson.

Twenty

The Sunroom is the kind of place that locks the doors when the rest of the country draws the curtains. I sat nodding in a corner with Hamilton's parcel on my lap, nursing ginger ales while the smoke pickled my tubes. The odd drifter made friendship noises and the spade started a query-list but I showed I was in no mood for a natter. It was light when the management started making bouncing moves so I dragged my feet through the wet on the pavements towards the public carsie in Leicester Square for a face-shine. The car was gone, thank Christ. There's an all night tea-stall near Charing Cross station so I called in for a bun and a cuppa, nudging a dosser and two fellers in evening dress. They were still pissed, the two Nigels, splashing wit like flat beer till the dosser, bent as a crone, started fingering their sleeves. They left straighter than they'd come and so did the dosser, who wasn't half as leprous without an audience. When a blue decked bogey turned up for a warmer I tucked the parcel under my arm and walked slow to the tube. Christmas is the time for prezzies and it was only just turned Easter. It takes two hours to travel right round the Circle Line and I did it twice on account of it's warmer than the zoo and three times as fascinating. You can predict where people will get off by the shape of their clothes when they get on.

I bought a twenty exposure FP3 at a chemists in the Swiss

Centre and was first inside when the Pavilion opened. Soon as the lights went down I hunched against the wall and checked the shooter. Government issue, with the two-inch barrel and a chamber showing five brass caps. I parked the box under the seat in front and dropped the revolver in the pocket of my windcheater. I never did figure what the picture was about. I jumped when somebody sat down behind me, the gold of his hair drawing the raindrops to my face, but it was just another swede. The auditorium was chocker, foreigners with no place to rest their plates. Full? I stood up. Six-thirty. The shooter thumped my ribs when I walked.

Two days.

I took a cab over London Bridge as far as Tooley Street and trod the rest of the way. Out on the road Minis jockeyed with meat-wagons while ravers from Kent rolled North to Saturday Night at the London Palladium, but the noise died round the first turning. The cobbles were rough and I picked careful between piles of rubble, one hand on the brickwork, head forward. The gap through Cooper's Yard fused grey in the air and lit the corners above the gates. The yard was bright, empty, echoing the engine of a boat. I kept to the wall, moving towards the wharf. The river was high, smelling bad and flowing fast. The crate-lid was where I'd left it. I did a circuit, checking the doors either side, then dragged a length of hoop-iron across the gap in the gates. The lights were showing across the river when I settled down to wait, and by half-eight it was dark. I tucked the Smith and Wesson in my jacket, hard against my belly.

The scrape of the hoop-iron had me on my feet and backing towards the river. Again. Somebody shuffled across the cobbles.

'Grant?'

Travis.

'Here.' I unbuttoned the windcheater, eyes raking the walls behind Travis. The river was noisy.

'Where is it?'

By focusing off-centre I could see the white of his face.

'Here.'

His hand wavered. 'Give it to me.' My heel touched the crate-lid. 'Give it to me.' Travis was playing his part like they were jammed in the aisles. But where was the audience?

'Give it to me!'

'Here.'

Travis's hand closed over the film. The hoop-iron tinkled but he didn't seem to hear. I backed off while he turned sideways, holding the spool close to his face.

'This isn't . . .'

The light from the gate soaked Travis white as he fumbled at his raincoat pocket.

'Now!' The voice was Hamilton's. 'Grant!'

Travis's face contorted at the voice, one arm raised against the light, pinned like a moth.

'*Both* of you?'

I fell on the crate lid as the shot clapped the walls. The impact flung Travis against the brickwork, his right hand trapped in his pocket, a paper cut-out outlined in black. His feet juddered forwards over the cobbles, shaking the body to a sitting position. His eyes were still open.

I was on my knees.

'Why?'

The light trembled, homing on Travis.

'Because,' McLeod dropped a revolver in his pocket, 'he was going to kill ye.'

Hamilton stood over me. 'Why didn't you shoot?'

'He . . .'

'Was going to kill you. Why didn't you shoot?'

'No. I mean . . . I didn't bring the shooter.'

McLeod had been fumbling with the body. 'He's dead.' He stood. 'C'mon, Harry. Get up.'

I held his arm, feet slithering.

'He would've shot you.' Hamilton looked at McLeod. 'Wouldn't he, Gordon?'

McLeod offered me a fag. 'Why d'ye not bring the gun,

Harry?'

'I . . . don't like shooters.'

I had bother keeping the cigarette still in my lips.

Hamilton sighed. 'You're not the man I thought you were. Show him, Gordon.'

McLeod bent over the corpse and felt in the raincoat pocket. Something fell out with the shooter.

'Now d'ye believe?' McLeod balanced the gun in his palm. The other article was a spectacles case, the specs Travis wore for reading. 'Ye saw him reach for his pocket, Harry. Ye owe me your life.'

I looked from one to the other, and I've never seen eyes so blank.

'Yeah.'

Hamilton spoke to McLeod.

'You'd better radio Collinson. We'll wait here.'

McLeod took the flashlight and slipped through the gates.

I coughed. 'Can I go?'

'In a few minutes. The police will want a statement.' Hamilton patted my shoulder. 'You'll be needed. It won't take very long, Harry.'

We watched the lights across the river.

'I sussed there wasn't no film.'

I couldn't see his face in detail. 'If you hadn't I'd have told you.' He sighed. 'There actually was a defector, you know. Travis knew that much. Unfortunately, the defector was . . . apprehended with the film on him. It was necessary to uphold the fiction, you see, because I had to force Travis into the open.' Hamilton looked at the shape sprawled on the cobbles. 'Pity.'

I shook my head. 'Stupid. He must've been stupid.'

'What made you change your mind? About the money, I mean? I'd describe that as a stroke of near genius, Harry. You knew I would've had no alternative. Why didn't you pursue it?'

I fumbled for a cigar. 'I . . .'

'You couldn't possibly have held it, of course. I'd have

seen to that.'

I felt for the capstan, cold iron under the wet of my hand. 'I figured just that. Decided to keep my nose clean.'

'Very wise.'

McLeod's flashlight hovered towards us.

'He's on his way.'

'Good.' Hamilton looked frail in the light of the torch. 'Now, before he gets here I'd like Harry to run over his statement. It's as well to clarify events in advance, don't you agree?'

I ran through the story, leaving out the bits he didn't know. Hamilton nodded.

'So you co-operated with the Bureau. Oh by the way, I think we can afford to omit your . . . slip of the tongue.' He sounded superior and confident. 'I daresay we owe Harry that much, Gordon?'

McLeod laughed. 'Nice try.'

'So.' Hamilton moved closer. 'You arranged the meeting with Travis. What happened at the meeting?'

I could hear McLeod breathing. 'Well, I'm waiting here and Travis comes through the gates. He says, have you got it, so I take the film out of my pocket. He scans it, then pulls a shooter. I think I'm dead till I hear you shout.' I swallowed. 'Just in time.'

'I don't think Harry's left anything out, do you, Gordon?'

It looked like a party over the river, all chains of lights and sounds of excitement we couldn't share. Then the walls outside the gates lit up and I heard the sound of a motor rumbling over the cobbles.

'Gordon. Show them in, will you?'

McLeod stood by the gates while three figures pushed through. They all carried flashlights and you could tell they were bogeys by the shape of their shoulders. Collinson walked to the body, his face hanging haggard from the brim of his hat.

Hamilton held out a hand. 'Jimmy.'

'Hullo, Roger.'

The other fuzz were nattering to McLeod, grouped round

the body. Travis sat as if waiting for somebody, feet apart and eyes open.

Hamilton coughed. 'I'm sorry.'

'Yes.' Collinson stooped and shut Travis's eyelids. 'I warned you.'

'I know. He would have killed Grant, you see.'

Collinson sighed. 'We needed to question him.'

'I'm sorry.'

'No choice.' He looked direct at Hamilton. 'I can square that part of it. But I wanted to talk to him.'

Hamilton looked thoughtful in the torchlight. 'It was probably too late, Jimmy.'

Collinson pushed his hat back and stepped away. 'Damned business.' He sighed. 'Can we use your office?'

McLeod's car was parked in Tooley Street well away from the area. We drove to Whitehall in convoy, me with McLeod, Hamilton in the fuzz-car with Collinson. The statements, as Collinson predicted, took some time. I said my piece several times over and by midnight I was shaking hands all round and promising to stay in touch if Collinson needed confirmation. It was finish-time for me, all buddy-buddy with the Law, everybody's favourite and the hero of the hour.

Collinson gave me a lift to Charlotte Street in the paddy-waggon, rabbitting away like it was all matter of course. I said yes or no as required but I kept thinking of Travis sitting there against the wall with his eyes open. What was it he'd said?

'*Both* of you?'

Politics is none of my business but I hate getting conned.

Twenty-one

I got Quist at nine in the morning.

'Where the bloody hell – '

'Got it?'

My voice cracked. 'Whaddaya think I been bloody calling you for?'

A pause. 'Don't call me again. I'll let you know soon as I've spoken to him.'

My fingers twitched. 'I gotta job of work to do first. It'll take a couple of hours.' My right eyelid kept closing. 'And Quist. I choose the spot. I'm not in the mood for chances, OK? You can tell him it's going to be somewhere open, somewhere I can see the bastard coming.'

I heard him sneer. 'What makes you think he'll do what you want?'

'If he wants the bread he'll meet me where I say. And get this. The gelt's not here, it's not round my gaff. So if anything happens to me he'll never get it.'

Down near the Elephant there's this pound for stray motors, ranks of jam-jars all locked in like lifers with a couple of screws minding the shop and collecting the snatch-money. There's nothing you can do about it. If the fuzz reckons you're parked in the wrong place they tow you away and if you don't roll the readies you don't get it back. I caught a bus down to the pound and walked a mile round the wall to the entrance.

It's an impressive sight, like a hypermarket in Orange County, motors nicked from every corner of the West End. I doddled down the lines and stomped into the office looking citizen-like which of course never fools the fuzz. This particular bogey was a kid with sideburns and hair long as he dared, which in the cavalry is an inch more than the average eunuch. He scanned my gear and I could see him thinking hullo all I need is one more pinch to make sergeant and this looks like it.

'Morning.' I was all charm and affability.

'Good morning, sir.'

I grinned. 'I gotta feeling you boys have taken my motor.' I gave him the number and he couldn't find it in the book. 'You must've got it.' My fingers tightened on the desk. 'Otherwise where is it?'

He looked me over. 'What did you say your name was, sir?'

'Grant. Harry Grant.' I tried to make my breathing look regular. 'It's a black 1300.' I laughed. 'I know you lads've got it tucked away somewhere.'

One day.

'Do you, sir?'

'Do me a favour. Take another look.'

'Did you check with Traffic Control, sir?'

'No. But it was parked in Leicester Square and . . .'

'Did you want the vehicle removed, sir?'

I snorted. 'Leave off.'

'What time did you park it?'

'About eight. Night before last.'

'Why didn't you ask for it when you found it was missing?'

I fought off the horrors. 'Ah well, I'd had a spot too much mother's so I reckoned it was best to catch a taxi home.'

'Suppose it had been there? Would you have driven the vehicle home, sir?'

'I'm not that daft, officer. Matter of fact I was just checking before I went home, know what I mean?' I leaned my elbows on the counter. 'I don't agree with drinking and driving.'

The bogey leafed through his ledger, shaking his head. I

clamped my hands together so they didn't shake.

His finger paused on a line. 'What did you say the number was?' I blurted so fast he flinched. 'No.' He paged on while I chewed my lip. 'Oh yes.'

'Yes?'

'We've got it.' His eyes wandered my face.

My laugh was like the sound of a sick horse. 'Told you.'

The fuzz wrote long and laboured in his book, filled out forms, stamped this and signed that, all with the speed of a man in deep space. Then he shoved a clip-board across the counter.

'Sign here.'

My name came out like a spider's footprints after a night in a saucer of scotch.

'What did you say your name was?'

'Grant.'

He printed it under my signature. 'Twenty-six pounds, sir.'

I dropped my wallet and scattered quiddies into his hand. He wrote a receipt like a four-year-old Borstal case.

'Log book, sir.' I gave it to him. 'Driving licence.' He watched my fingers. 'Insurance certificate, MOT certificate.' He inspected them all one by one, then searched the mass of tickets at his elbow.

'Row H. Fifteenth car along.'

I had to sit inside the car for ten minutes till I felt well enough to drive.

I could hear the phone ringing in the gaff soon as I opened the street door. Quist.

'He says five o'clock tomorrow.'

'Suits me.'

'In the morning.'

'What?'

'That's what he said. You choose the place, he says the time. Where?'

I'd thought that through. 'Primrose Hill, at the top, near the benches.'

I could almost hear him smirk.

'Trust him, do you?'

'Sure I trust him. In the middle of fifty acres of green grass.'

'If I don't call assume it's on.'

It was time to plan for old age. I dragged my case off the wardrobe and dropped what was left of Cheryl-Jo's giftie in the bottom. Then I packed careful, starting with socks. The Smith and Wesson was still in the pocket of my windcheater. I sat on the bed, cradling it in my hands, then shoved it in my waistband, buttoned my jacket and carried the pigskin bag downstairs. Bishop came out of the shop.

'Leaving, Mr Grant?'

I straightened. 'What do I owe you?'

'A week.' He looked sad. 'Wish you'd said. Now I've got to go through the whole business again.'

I gave him the money. 'Short let, right? You can't expect ten years' notice.'

When he left I stowed the bag in the back seat of the car and tucked the shooter in the glove compartment. Then I called into the shop.

'Leave the door ajar, right? I'm coming down with a case.'

Bishop nodded.

I stood in the gaff, suitcase in hand, thinking it had left more scars on me than I had on it. A last check, and I turned to the door. The phone started crowing like a blood-crazed bantam.

'Harry?'

'Christ.' The Major. 'I forgot.'

'So it seems. I've been trying to raise you for days.'

'Look – '

'Don't apologize, old chap, just listen.' The Major was in control. 'It concerns a friend of ours . . .' There was only one friend we had in common these days. My fingers tightened on the receiver.

'You seen him? Crab? Our *friend*?'

'I use the word advisedly, Harry.' The Major paused. 'He admires you.'

I sneered. 'Yeah – '

'I mean what I say. Crab came to see me when I returned from Beirut. He asked for help.' He waited. 'He told me about Quist. I know everything. Harry. Try to understand Crab's position . . .'

I hollered. 'If he got you to phone up just to – '

'He had no choice. He came to me because he wanted to make amends.'

'Great,' I jeered, 'and you – '

'Harry. You've been had.'

'Say again.'

He spoke slow.

'Quist has never met Cain.'

The walls reeled.

'Harry?'

'I'm . . . yeah.'

'Crab asked if I might be able to reach Cain. Are you listening? Crab . . . doesn't care for Sergeant Quist.' He breathed slow and regular down the phone. 'Men like Cain are not . . . easy to find. But, well, modesty prevents me from boasting about my contacts in . . . er, shall we say, hardware . . . A colleague of mine knew somebody who . . .' I listened to him light a fag. 'My colleague tells me Mister Cain is, er, put out by Quist. He wishes a word with him. He'll have it eventually whether you help or not.' He coughed quietly. 'After all, he has a certain . . . reputation to protect, n'est-ce pas?' I was struggling to keep up.

'What . . . what about the gelt? Did Crab tell you about the money I nicked off Cain?'

'Let's put it this way.' The Major chose his words. 'No names have been mentioned. Only Quist. The money hasn't been discussed. But Harry . . . if you'll forgive me, it was rather stupid of you. The money is a problem you will eventually have to face. From what my, er, colleague tells me, Mister Cain is not the sort to have forgotten that episode.' A long pause. 'Quist will never leave you alone, Harry. Crab knows him well. Interesting how events . . . converge, isn't it?'

I had no choice, and nothing to lose.

'Tell your mate I'm meeting Quist at Primrose Hill, five tomorrow morning.'

I heard him stand up straight.

'Good show.'

'Quist's too fly to show unless he sees me first.' I wiped my face with a handkerchief. 'Five o'clock. Tell your friend.'

'Good luck, old man.'

'Major. Thanks.'

I stumbled into the gaff and sat on the bed.

I don't know how long I sat staring at my hands, but when I raised my head Felix was leaning on the door.

'It wasn't locked.'

She wore a straight skirt and a vee-necked sweater, hair drawn into a bun that stretched the skin on her cheek-bones. She shut the door and leaned on the panels. Her face was pale.

'Come in.'

'Are you leaving?'

I collected what was left of my thoughts. 'Even us scum gotta take holidays. Thought I'd spend a few days in the sun. Spain, maybe.'

She stepped into the middle of the room, hands in her skirt pockets, and glanced at my suitcase. 'You're all of a piece, Willie. Not a hair, not a thought out of character.'

'The name's Harry.'

'Harry.' She tapped my case with her toe. 'Do you know I found out only yesterday what you did at the Alhambra? The bottles of water?'

I lit a cigar. 'Well I don't suppose the average scrubber is privy to the management's minutes, is she?'

'No.' She came closer. 'I wish they'd told me before, though. I admire you. It showed nerve.'

'Well, we all gotta make a living, haven't we?'

'What a pity you're so small-minded. You have talent.'

I reached for my case. 'We can't all be bold, love. Some of my best friends were bold and now they're resting under the lawn not a million miles from Golders Green. I'll stay scared, thanks.'

'Lacey was arrested, you know.'

'Lacey?'

'The steam-room deepened his burns. He had to give himself up.'

I sat down. 'You know what your crumpet did to him?'

'Beau was proud.' She shrugged. 'Lacey made a fool of him. He got what he deserved.'

'Christ.' I almost laughed. 'Out of my way. I'm busy.'

'He was a friend of yours, wasn't he?'

'Who?'

'Lacey.'

'Not so's you'd notice.'

'You set Beau up.'

'Wrong again. I was trying to get the Fabergé.' I looked at her. 'Come to think of it, I'd tell you it was Hamilton that sent Lacey to the sauna but you wouldn't believe me. Stay clear and keep your head down, that's the Grant family motto translated from the Latin. It's kept me out of bother so far and I don't intend switching tracks now.'

'You're very convincing, Willie.' She sat on the bed. 'Harry. Whatever your name is.'

'The boyfriend couldn't help me dead, darlin. I was busy looking for Hamilton's film, remember?'

'Ah.' She lay back on her elbows, knees together. 'Roger's conjuring-trick. Who won?'

'Doesn't Sir Roger always win?'

'Always.'

Like I said, I hate to get conned. 'How much do you know about your friend Roger? I'd ask him a few questions if I was you. Ask him about Travis. You might've met Travis, young bloke, your sort, out of the Guards via Harrods. Poor old Travis wasn't the brightest of sparks. I mean, where he came from officers played cricket and paid their debts, so naturally when he smells something bad he keeps batting careful but makes signals to the captain. Trouble is the captain doesn't seem to notice, and the very next ball belts Travis smack between the eyes. Funny thing, the captain shakes hands with the bowler and they leave the field together. Any of this make sense to you?'

She yawned. 'No.'

I grabbed her wrists. 'Sit up, I'm telling you something!' I talked fast. 'Ask Sir Roger about Cohen, eh? Ask him if Travis and me needed convincing that bad, I mean, was it worth it? Or was he just trying to stop Travis sussing there was no film? Uncle Roger needed bait, he needed me to draw Travis to the hook, and there's more, so bloody well look at me when I'm talking to you. He wanted someone to pull the trigger for him, someone he'd scared so he'd blast a hole in brick at the sound of boo. Only he made a bad judgement. But he's so bloody smart he worked it right in the end anyway. You listening?'

She stood, smoothing the creases in her skirt. 'You bore me.' She turned at the door. 'I invited some friends of yours, I hope you don't mind.' She turned the knob and stood aside, quiet and poised. 'I know they want to see you, anyway.'

Fat Man, Percy and Golly came in like clowns out of a circus car, fanning out round the bed.

Felix smiled. 'Thank you for seeing me, Willie.'

I sighed. 'Harry.'

'Remember me to Roger.' She smiled again as she shut the door.

Golly stepped back till his shoulders rested on the door-jamb, arms folded across his chest. The bed sagged under Fat Man's weight.

He shook his head. 'Willie.'

'Harry.' I took off my jacket. 'How you been?'

Percy limped up and down the mat, chin tucked into his chest, right shoulder making twitches.

'So-so,' said Fat Man. 'You?'

I backed towards the window, rolling my shirt-sleeves. 'You know, grabbing a crust where I can.'

'You upset me, Willie.' Fat Man wobbled his chins. 'It took me a whole week to feel normal again.'

'Harry. Feel better now, though, do you?'

Golly giggled into his hand. 'Hey, man. What for you taking off your jacket?'

I winked. 'Force of habit. I hate getting stains on my gear. Specially that. It cost a hundred dollars.' My heels touched the wall as Fat Man heaved upright. 'Be gentle, boys,' I told them. 'Remember I'm a virgin.'

Twenty-two

Bishop found me on the landing just as I'd decided it was peaceful lying still. He cleaned me up and fed me tots from a bottle while we waited for the ambulance. I could walk as long as the ambulance men were in reach, and managed to stop awake in the back of the wagon as far as the Middlesex. They shipped me into Casualty, filled my arm with something from a needle and did what repairs they could. It looked like I wouldn't be playing wing for Chelsea next season after all. I came to about three-thirty shouting Cain and fumbling for my gear. A nurse came running but I was in no mood for lectures. By the time she'd fetched the houseman I was sort of dressed, but believe me if you're right-handed it isn't all tea and crumpets when you've only got your left.

'Mr Grant. Please get back into bed.'

I turned, slow as Boris with the bolt through his neck. 'Can't. I've got my best suit on.'

He took my elbow. 'Please. You're not fit enough.'

'Get off!'

He stepped back, all proper in his nice white coat. 'Have it your own way. Please sign your discharge.'

I limped to the night-desk and gave up trying to read the form on the second line. 'Where?' The nurse poked a pen into my fingers and I scrawled something at the bottom. 'How do I vacate this flesh-factory?'

The houseman helped me to the lift.

The Middlesex is one block from Charlotte Street and that was far enough. It was dark and deserted apart from the odd raver going home from a party, and I had to stop five times on the way. It took time to find the key with my left hand. I let myself in and took a breather every other step, trying to ease the sling so my right arm didn't knock my ribs. The gaff was a mess. Splintered table, bedclothes on the floor, stains on the wall near the window. Working with one hand, stopping every ten seconds, I collected what was left and dropped them in my case, sponge-bag, toothbrush, shaving gear. One last look. I dropped the keys on the bed and let the suitcase slide while I took the stairs one at a time.

The motor stood cold at the kerb. Movements had to be split into separate actions, and every time I turned lightning struck me in the chest. I shoved the case in the back, climbed careful into the driver's seat and waited for the mist to clear from my eyes while the engine warmed. Slowly into second, away from the kerb, trying not to jerk or stall, a steady fifteen miles an hour in second gear with one hand on the wheel. I trundled down Great Percy Street and into Tottenham Court Road, taking care over the junction at the top, ready to stop on amber. There wasn't much traffic on Hampstead Road, a few lorries headed for the M1 but I wasn't offering competition. I held an eye wide for signs of fuzz who might be interested in a pile of bandages driving a car with one hand at that time of the dark. Into the back streets at Mornington Crescent, nice and slow round Regent's Park Road, up the hill and left at Elsworthy Road. There's a cul-de-sac called Elsworthy Terrace that butts into the grass on Primrose Hill. I stopped against the gates at the end.

It took effort to get the boot open and drop the spare on the road, and light was reflecting blank off the windows of the houses behind me by the time I'd loosened the tyre. I leaned against the car, head down till my chest stopped heaving. The wrench was useful because it allowed me to scoop the bundles one by one without bending. In the back seat I emptied the pigskin bag, collected the notes and packed them tight. I slung the spare in the boot, leaning on the window watching the reflection of my mouth. The shooter lay quiet and shiny in the glove compartment. I opened the door, shoved the gun into the sling on my right arm, hefted the pigskin and stepped into the park. It was ten to five.

It was a long plod up the path. When I reached the crest the sky was luminous grey, the bench was cold and wet, and the noises I could hear were coming from my own throat.

Primrose Hill looks clear over Regent's Park, a sort of knuckle between St John's Wood and Camden Town. The North side is wooded but the South rolls green all the way to the Zoo so if your visitor comes from the South you can watch him for maybe five minutes, depending how fit he is. The light was getting better but it wasn't giving twenty-twenty and for that reason I missed the first signs. I saw him when he'd covered about a third, a shadow wading the damp. I sat still, judging the distance, the weight of the shooter on my arm. The figure wavered like a rock in a heat-haze, changed course and headed towards me. I stood up.

Quist.

He was out of breath, head bent, a slick of hair hanging off his scalp. He stopped ten yards away. I turned, wincing, searching the trees on the North. Quist caught his breath.

'Keep still. D'you want to get us both killed?'

'Where is he?'

He wiped his mouth on his sleeve. 'Jesus. That was a hard climb.'

I cast about, the trees spinning round my head.

'Just act normal.' Quist moved closer. 'Had an accident? You don't look well.'

The sun touched the Post Office tower like fire to a fuse.

'Where – '

'Where's the gelt?' My feet slipped on the grass till we stood on the same level. 'This it?' Quist drew the pigskin bag from my hand, watching my face. 'This the money?' He poked boney fingers into the flap. The sun lanced at the tips of the trees and flung shadows across the grass. Quist slung the bag under his arm and drew his lips over stained teeth. 'You'll be all right now, Harry. I should go if I was you.'

I tucked my left hand into the sling, moving down the slope so Quist turned his back on the trees.

'He'll . . . I mean, he knows it's from me?'

'Who?'

As the sun flushed Quist's face something moved in the shadow of the trees behind him.

'Cain.'

'Oh him.'

A man was standing at the edge of the wood.

'Fact is, I dunno where he is.' Quist scratched his nose. 'See . . .' his shoulders twitched, 'I only heard about him secondhand. Oh, Carson told me about you and Cain all right, but I never went looking for this Cain. Just your mate Crab. That was enough.' Quist's mouth stretched and formed a silent hole that showed his fillings while laughter glistened in the corners of his eyes. 'You've been conned, Harry, you know that, don't you? And the best of it is . . . who'll believe you?' He bent at the waist, wheezing, hair slipping forwards over his skull. 'Mister Cain. Oh Christ, you bloody fool.' He wiped his eyes while I tried not to watch the figure at the edge of the trees. 'Don't take it to heart, boy. Everyone's got his Mister Cain if you're smart enough to spot it.' He patted his gut, chuckling. 'Anyway, thanks for coming through so prompt.' He stepped awkwardly down the slope, bald, the hair above his right ear swinging to his shoulder.

I looked up. The man by the trees had started to move. He walked easily, graceful, hands at his sides, head reflecting the first rays of the sun. My fingers tightened on the Smith and Wesson. Cain stopped, eyes settling on my sling.

I lifted my chin. 'That's . . . Quist.'

He glanced at the figure on the slope, then back to my arm. Dew splashed off the polish of his shoes as he stepped forward, distended the edge of my sling with one finger and unhooked the shooter. He opened the chamber and spilled the five rounds into the palm of his hand.

'That's Quist,' I said again. The calm eyes watched Quist stumble on the grass. 'He's got your money.' I swallowed. 'Maybe you don't recognize me. Grant. The Carson job.'

'I know.' He extended the butt of the Smith and Wesson towards my hand. 'Don't make a fool of yourself, Grant.' I started to walk up the hill.

When I looked over my shoulder Quist was stumbling about twenty yards from the gates. Cain's shadow glided over the grass towards him, silent, final. I threw the shooter into the trees and turned back the way I'd come. The Major would be expecting a drink.